Dreams
Of
Ivory

CARRIE ANN RYAN

DEDICATION

To Rebecca Royce. Thanks so much for believing in me.

ACKNOWLEDGMENTS

Thank you Lia Davis. You always know when to kick me in the pants and get me moving. Thanks for loving Jackson as much as I do.

Thank you Devin. You totally knew how to make Honor find herself. You are the best editor ever.

Thanks Fatin and Lillie. You're help and support means everything to me.

Thank you Charity for loving the Cooper Brothers as much as I do.

And finally, thank you readers for picking this one up and the ones before it. I couldn't do this without you.

CHAPTER 1

"Maybe if he got laid, he wouldn't be such an ass."

Jackson Cooper gritted his teeth as the words floated into the grocery store aisle. He gripped the handle on his cart then took a deep breath. He had two choices: either confront the woman who'd spoken or walk past her and act like the ass he knew he was.

The latter seemed like the best choice since he really didn't give two cents about an opinion from a woman he'd turned down.

Twice.

He put the box of pasta on the bottom of his cart and moved down the aisle, passing Jessica Turnip's—the woman who'd spoken—and Claudia Sanders' wide-eyed looks.

"Oh, J-Jackson..." Jessica stuttered, her too-painted cheeks blushing, her heavily shadowed-eyes wide with mocking and just a bit of fear. "It's good to see you. Um...I wasn't talking about you...no...it was..."

Her voice trailed off as she clutched her throat—as if he'd strangle her for her comments.

Really? They'd been talking about another Jackson Cooper who happened to be a dentist?

The two gossips had been talking about how the single male pool had almost completely dried up in Holiday, Montana with the sudden marriages of the Cooper brothers. Well, at least four of the five brothers. It'd be a cold day in hell if he ever took that plunge. When they'd come to his name in the short list of available men, Claudia had giggled while Jessica had sighed.

Apparently they wanted him, and he wanted nothing to do with them.

Hence why they thought he was an ass.

Well, he was an ass, but he had good reasons—he didn't particularly like people.

He just didn't care about being nice for the sake of making people feel better about their own jealousy and insecurities.

Instead of saying what was really on his mind though, he merely raised a cool brow then turned his back to them, walking toward the check-out lines. He heard their mumbled voices as he left, but he didn't bother trying to figure out what they were saying. Either they were commenting on his ass or the fact that he was an ass.

Most likely both.

Hell, he missed having his brothers free to be able to take the brunt of the female population, but now they'd all married within a short time of each other. Matt and Jordan had married first, soon after they'd gotten back together. Then Justin, Tyler, and Brayden had married the loves of their lives in a triple ceremony on the Cooper property.

Though the whole town had tried to come, Jackson and the women were having none of that. No, everyone had wanted a small

ceremony with only family and close friends.
Even Jackson's cousins had come into town,
his cousin Caleb bringing his two girls to be
flower girls along with Lacy, Brayden's new
daughter. Brayden's two new sons, Cameron
and Aiden, had been ring bearers while
Jackson had stood awkwardly to the side acting
like best man and maid of honor.

Apparently that had been the women's
wishes, so he'd done it, but he'd be damned if
he let anyone other than his family mention the
fact. It was either that, or let the women bring
in another woman to take the job and match
make.

Hell no.

Everyone had wanted the ceremony to
be fast yet peaceful, so they had done just that
back in March. Brayden and Allison had been
dating for little more than two weeks before
they got married, but really; they'd been
circling around each other for ten years, so it
hadn't seemed fast for any of them. Tyler and
Abigail had been the same way with their fast
courtship. The two had known each other for
years and were perfect for each other. Seeing
how Tyler was a cupid, it only made sense his
brother would know his own mind.

Well, that was as long as Tyler didn't have a curse on him, but that was a whole other story.

Justin and Rina had known each other the shortest amount of time, but it didn't seem to bother them that they were now shackled to each other.

As long as they left Jackson's personal life alone, he'd stay on the sidelines and watch the happy newlyweds gush and smile at each other for eternity. Yet, it was the odd gleams in their eyes when they looked at him that made him worry. They were either filled with pity that he was alone or were calculating how to make him join their wedded bliss.

Again, not for him.

Ever.

He'd made it to the checkout line when his phone rang. With a sigh, he checked the screen and answered Matt's call.

"Yes?" he asked, his voice clipped. Not that he was angry with Matt, but if his brother was calling now, it was probably for an errand Jackson wasn't in the particular mood to do.

"Hey, bro, we need a favor," Matt said,

his voice a little harried.

We.

Ah yes, we. That either meant him and Jordan, or him and the rest of the Coopers. Jackson never knew anymore since they all congregated together far too often. Not that he didn't love his brothers and new sisters-in-law. He just felt that being alone and at peace would be nice every once in a while.

"Yes?" he said again, ignoring the looks of Jessica and Claudia as they passed him again.

"We need peanut butter. A lot of peanut butter."

Jackson blinked. "Uh, don't you already have some at home?"

Matt let out a shaky laugh. "Yes, but it's not the right brand and right now all four women are at the house picking wallpaper and craving peanut butter."

Jackson let out another sigh. "What kind?"

"I knew you'd help. Thanks, Jacks. Okay, Jordan wants the extra crunchy kind. Rina wants smooth. Abby wants that New Age organic kind with honey inside, and Allison wants the kind with the jelly already added. You know those mini Coopers. They're picky."

Jackson blinked again, almost at a loss for words as he ignored the mini Cooper reference, a term the girls loved and had begun calling their offspring. Having four women all entering the second trimester of their pregnancy at the same time was just about killing the brothers. How the hell had he become part of this? He wasn't married to any of them, and yet now he was the peanut butter bearer.

Hell.

"Four...four types of peanut butter?" Jackson asked.

"Yes. Four. I'm alone in the house with four pregnant women who all want peanut butter of their own choosing. For the love of God, help me."

The panic in his brother's voice made Jackson smile. Matt had the pre-daddy jitters. In fact, all his brothers did.

"Fine. I'll get out of line and get your peanut butter, but there's no way in hell I'm getting out of my car to drop them off. You'll have to come out—sans women. I need to get to work since I took the morning off."

Matt laughed. "I still can't believe you did that. I called your office first to see if you'd pick some up on your way home, and your receptionist was there doing paperwork and told me you'd be in late. I thought hell had frozen over."

Jackson gritted his teeth as he made his way to the peanut butter aisle. He still couldn't believe there were so many types of it. He piled them into his cart and shook his head.

"I had a cracked bicuspid emergency last night and didn't get home until late. I decided I could take off the morning since my appointments were easily moved."

The perks of a small town was that he could afford to change things around if his loyal patients were on the books.

The downside was that he was the only dentist in town—as well as the county. He never got a break unless he inconvenienced someone.

"I'm not blaming you, Jacks, God no. It's about time you take time for yourself."

Jackson rolled his eyes and made his way back to the checkout lines—this time four jars of peanut butter heavier. "I'm fine with the way things are, Matt."

"If you say so, Jacks. Okay, I'll be on the lookout for your car and will run out to you so you can speed off before the women come out. I'll make the excuse that you have to head to work. Which really isn't a lie since it's your favorite thing to do."

Jackson grunted at his brother's remark then hung up without saying goodbye. Matt would get the gist of it. He paid and made his way to his car, ignoring the looks of his townspeople. The Coopers were the most well known family in all of Holiday, so it wasn't surprising he garnered a few looks.

Plus he was a single man in a town full of single women.

God, he needed a vacation away from Holiday.

When he got to Matt and Jordan's place, he parked near the curb but didn't go to the driveway. He needed a quick escape in case one of the women saw him. Considering one was a witch, another a magical elf, and one more like a harpy, he wasn't taking any chances. Not to mention that Allison was raising three children with another on the way and was as fierce as any momma bear.

Yeah, he wasn't too afraid to admit—to himself—that he'd steer clear of the new Coopers as long as possible.

The front door opened, and Matt ran out, his hair standing on end as though he'd been running his hands through it throughout the day. Considering he'd been in the house alone with four pregnant women all day, Jackson couldn't blame him.

"Oh thank God," Matt said as he took the bag from Jackson. "They're all upstairs looking at more wallpaper for one of the guest rooms. Jordan is going crazy with finishing renovations on the house, but don't tell her I said that." His eyes widened as if he'd just noticed what he'd let slip.

Jackson let out a deep chuckle. "Your words are safe with me. Is everyone off work today?"

Matt raised a brow. "It's Saturday, Jacks. They're all off work and bugging me. Again, don't tell them I said that. Brayden and

Justin took the kids on a hike near your place, and Tyler is on duty today while he trains his new deputy, Hugh."

Jackson ran a hand through his own hair. "Hell, I don't even know what day it is anymore."

Matt looked over his shoulder at the house then nodded. "Take time for yourself, Jacks. You're only thirty-eight, yet you're looking far too haggard for a thirty-eight-year-old man. I need to get back before they come out."

Jackson glared but nodded. "After your charming words on my appearance, I don't know how I'll be able to leave your company."

Matt laughed then walked backward toward the house. "Get some rest, though we both know you'll ignore me. We have a guys' night out soon, so don't forget."

Jackson waved him off and drove toward his own home to take care of his groceries. The Cooper brothers had regular guys' nights out, though now they were down to maybe twice a month with everyone getting married. He enjoyed the time with his family, though he would never confess it. He might be an ass according to some people, but he loved his family more than they knew.

They were the ones who kept him going since he had little else to do it for him.

It took him a bit to get to his house since he was right on the outskirts of town in the woods. His house—the Cooper place—had been his parents' home before they died. He held back the usual shudder that came with that though, and as the eldest son, Jackson had been the one to inherit the house. All his brothers called it his place, but he'd never thought of it that way.

No, it would always be the Cooper place. His name might be on the deed, but his brothers and their families were always welcome.

He put away his groceries then headed back out to work. He always wore slacks and a button-down shirt unless he would be staying home. Then it was jeans and a shirt, so he didn't have to change to go to work.

As much as he wanted to go to work because it was his life, he honestly didn't know if he could take those steps into the building. He really just wanted to take a nap, but he knew that wouldn't be possible.

Jackson walked into his office and nodded to his receptionist, a pretty blonde who, thankfully, was married and didn't hit on him. He wasn't vain but, hell, it was hard to be the only single Cooper left. Maybe he should invite his cousins Chase and Caleb to move in so he wouldn't be the only one. Caleb, though, was a recent widower, so Jackson wasn't sure if he was even ready to date.

He went through his normal routine, looking through his emails and charts, getting ready for the day. It was odd to start in the middle of the day, rather than at the crack of dawn, but he'd needed the time to get groceries and sleep. He hadn't had a day off in two weeks, and because he was open weekends to accommodate his working patients, he'd been at his wit's end.

After three fillings and a child's checkup, Jackson made his way back to his office, his temples throbbing. Nothing a little coffee wouldn't fix. His two hygienists were working on cleanings so he'd have to go and finish the checkups soon.

As he took a sip of the dark brew from his fancy one-cup maker—his one splurge—he closed his eyes, trying to regain the energy he'd had as a man in his twenties and early thirties, rather than the man who was on the downhill slide to the dreaded forty.

Hell, he wasn't ready to hit forty.

Wasn't he supposed to have his whole life ahead of him? Yet, here he was, alone and a workaholic, watching as his magical younger brothers found the loves of their lives and were making a future for themselves.

Not that he wanted the wife and kids, but a future beyond work would be nice.

And he definitely didn't want their magical abilities.

Holiday, Montana, seemed to be the mecca of holiday paranormals, and the Coopers were so deeply entrenched in it, Jackson wasn't sure how he'd been spared. They had witches, Santa's elves and executives, cupids, leprechauns, harpies, and ghosts. Even his new nephews and niece were half-gnome.

Magic and the paranormal seemed to touch everything in his life, and he was so dammed grateful he'd been spared.

Jackson hated magic.

Hated it all.

With magic came instability and the possibility of things he'd rather not think about. Enemies came with those powers, and one never knew when such an enemy would pop up and try to destroy it all. He'd had to watch as his brothers had been almost taken down one by one by magic forces, and Jackson had been helpless to fight against it.

He was the only Cooper untouched by magic, and he'd be damned if he'd let it happen to him.

There was a knock on the door and he looked up as his receptionist, Veronica, stuck her head in, an odd expression on her face.

"Yes?" he asked, annoyed his moment of peace was now over.

"Uh, Dr. Cooper, there's a woman out there who says she needs to speak with you, but she doesn't have an appointment."

Jackson didn't miss the curiosity in her gaze, but he ignored it. "Did she say exactly what she wanted?"

Veronica shook her head. "No, but she said it was personal. She also doesn't look like one of those Cooper groupies, so I thought I'd ask you anyway." She winked, and Jackson held back a smile.

"Did she say what her name was?" he asked, a little bit of that curiosity peeking through his stubbornness.

"Honor. Honor Bridges."

Jackson coughed up the sip of coffee he'd taken then cursed as he spilled some on his shirt. Veronica's eyes widened, and she stepped in the office. He held up his hand.

"I've got it. Hell, tell her to give me a minute while I change my shirt."

His receptionist looked as though she desperately wanted to question his reaction and the fact that he wanted to talk to this woman, but she thankfully held her tongue.

"If you say so."

He turned his back to her to grab a new shirt from his closet, and she left, closing the door behind her. As he buttoned up his new shirt, he tried to stop his fingers from shaking.

What the hell was Honor doing here?

He hadn't seen her in...almost eight

years.

He rolled his shoulders and made his way to the door. He'd just get this over with. There wasn't anything between them—there hadn't been for too long. He'd just nod and say hello to an old...friend...then get back to his day.

She stood in his waiting room facing the wall so he only saw her profile, and damn if he didn't lose his breath.

She had to be at least in her early thirties now, but she looked at least a decade younger. Her long black hair fell to the middle of her back, straight, yet thick and exotic. He could remember how soft it had felt against his chest late at night.

She turned to him then, and he set his face so he wouldn't gasp. Her striking blue eyes had always called to him, and now was no different. Since she was average height, her curves suited her well, her hips just wide enough for his hands...

No, not the time.

It would never be the time.

Her face was elegant, her cheekbones

sharp, but not too sharp, her chin pointed like an elfish goddess.

Hell, she looked even more beautiful now than she had eight years ago.

Honor would have to go.

Soon.

"Honor," he said, his voice surprisingly steady despite the emotions warring through him.

"Jackson," she said, her smile making her whole face brighten.

Veronica stood between them, her gaze traveling between the two.

"I had called before, but you didn't say anything," Honor said, but Jackson didn't say anything back.

He remembered her first call months ago, and the few calls afterward, but he'd never said anything back, thinking it couldn't have been her—shouldn't have been her.

She couldn't be here...not the one who'd left him.

No, he didn't want to think about the

past.

"Um..." She looked down at her hands as she wrung them together then squared her shoulders. "I just wanted to say that I'm staying at the inn."

He swallowed hard and nodded. "You're visiting your aunt then?"

Honor shook her head. "No, I'm staying here in Holiday, Jackson. That's what I wanted to say when I called and why I'm here. I know it's been forever, and you don't care, but I thought I'd say it anyway."

"You're moving here?" he asked, his voice hoarse.

No, hell no. She couldn't move here. Holiday was his home, and there was no way he could share it with her.

"Yes, I'm staying. I left before because..." She shook her head. "No, that doesn't matter, not anymore. I'm here to stay though. My aunt needs me, and I have responsibilities that I've been ignoring too long."

He didn't know what kind of responsibilities she could possibly have since she'd been gone for eight years, but he ignored it. "Why can't your brother, Tucker, help?"

Surprise then hurt crossed her face. She must have been surprised that he'd remembered her brother's name, and he cursed himself for letting that slip. For a woman he was supposed to have forgotten, he remembered too much about her.

The hurt was obvious, but he couldn't show that he cared.

"Tucker's busy," she said shortly. "I'm sorry to take your time, but I wanted to tell you I was in town."

"Why should I care?" he asked, trying to put distance between them.

He ignored the gasp from Veronica and cursed himself for being so rude. He'd forgotten they had an audience. The news of this confrontation would be all over Holiday's grapevine as soon as Honor walked out the door.

Honor rolled her eyes and smiled. Hell, he'd never understood this woman. "Whatever, Jackson. Play the stoic man if you want, but I wanted to tell you anyway. Bye."

She turned on her heel and walked out

of his practice, her hips swaying, leaving him breathless.

He forced his gaze to Veronica and frowned. "I take it there's no way I can make you keep this between us?"

"Huh?" she asked as she looked up from texting on her phone.

He shook his head. "Never mind. Let me know when my next appointment shows up."

Jackson left Veronica to her gossip and closed himself in his office.

Honor was back.

What the hell was he going to do now?

CHAPTER 2

Honor Bridges ran her hand through her hair and cursed herself. It had been over three hours since she'd left Jackson's office, and she was still shaking. It had been eight years, and the man still made her want to jump him and never let go.

He might act all stoic and broody, but she knew he could smile—that he could feel.

Well, at least he had eight years ago when she'd known him. Honestly, she didn't know this new Jackson at all. For all she knew, he'd encased himself in even more ice than he'd had before and was such a complete ass he didn't have a feeling in him.

His words had stung, but she quickly got over them. She'd seen the look in his eyes when she'd turned to him. It was fury, confusion, arousal, and hurt all rolled into one. Though he'd masked it quickly, she'd seen it.

It gave her hope, though, hope for what she had no idea.

It wasn't as though she wanted to get back together with him—not that they'd been truly together before. She had only wanted to let him know she was there because she hadn't wanted it to be a surprise, though, in retrospect, that seemed a bit self-centered and foolish.

She'd been so afraid he wouldn't have even remembered her, and then she'd seen the way he'd looked at her. She'd called him those few times before, but he'd acted as though he didn't know who she was, but he'd known her name—and her brother's name.

He'd remembered.

For some reason, that made her feel all warm and giddy inside.

Not that she'd do anything about it.

Honor was back in Holiday because she

had a job to do. She'd neglected it for so long and had only been able to do so because of who her aunt was. Shame flooded her, but she pressed it down. She'd do what was right and get over herself and her past.

After all, she was a tooth fairy and there were little kids who needed her and the hope she'd bring with her job, but she'd get back to that soon. Her aunt would help her get acclimated, and she'd find her way.

She just had to get out of her room and get on with her life.

The sun beat down on her as she walked out of the inn, passing the innkeeper on her way. Connie seemed like her own fairy godmother. The woman always seemed to know what she needed and when. Honor put on her sunglasses and tilted her face to the sun, needing its energy and warmth to do what she had to.

Her aunt was waiting for her, and she'd put this off long enough.

She hadn't stayed with her aunt because they were both old enough that they needed their own space.

A shout made her turn, and then a heavy

object pushed her to the ground, skinning her hands and bare knees.

"What the hell?" She gasped and turned, she was laying under a hard body. Honor tried to push off the warm weight and winced as her palms burned. She blinked as she looked into Jackson's deep blue eyes, filled with fear.

"Are you okay?" he asked as he looked down at her. He knelt above her, lifting his weight off her body, then ran his large hands up and down her sides.

She pressed down the heat her libido seemed to love and pushed him away. "Why did you knock me down?"

He frowned at her then stood, bringing her up with him. "You've hurt your knees and palms. Let's go in and get Connie to help me clean them out."

Honor pushed him away again, ignoring the sting in her cuts. She looked up at the man who towered over her at over six feet and narrowed her eyes, taking in his thick hair. It was cropped to his head, a little bit of gray coloring his temples.

Heck, he looked hotter now than he had before.

Her nipples pressed against her sundress, and she fought not to rub up along the man like a cat in heat.

No, no, totally not the time.

"You don't get to tell me what to do, and why the hell did you push me? Didn't get enough barbs in before so you decided to push me down instead?"

She winced at the look of hurt that crossed his face before he schooled his expression again. "I'll let that one go since you're clearly addled from your near-miss."

She opened her mouth to say something about that, but he shook his head and moved out of the way so she could see the broken remains of what looked to be a large flowerpot on the ground. The ceramic lay in shattered pieces amongst the dirt and dying flowers.

"What...what?" She blinked, not knowing what to say.

"That was coming down for your head, so I pushed you out of the way. You could have been seriously hurt or killed, Honor."

Her palms went clammy as her body shook. She looked up to the open window but didn't see anyone. "I guess it just fell..."

Jackson followed her gaze then nodded. "Accidents happen, but hell Honor, that scared the shit out of me."

She smiled, despite what had happened. "If I'd had time to react, I guess it would have scared the shit out of me too."

He smiled at her, and her heart melted. Damn, the man was one sexy Cooper. The mummers of voices around her made her aware of the crowd they'd collected.

Connie came running to them, tears running down her checks. "Oh, Honor, are you all right? Thank God Jackson was walking by when that happened." The inn was near his office, so it made sense he'd be around. "I have no idea how that fell. I keep my pots far away from the ledge. Oh, Honor, I'm so sorry."

Honor gave the woman a hug, ignoring her hurts, and squeezed tight. "I'm fine. Jackson's the hero here."

Jackson grunted and pushed Honor away slightly. "I'm just lucky I was here when I was." He turned toward the crowd. "We're fine, give her some space." At the sound of his stern voice, some of the gawkers left, and Honor ignored the rest. "Let's get you inside so we can look at your palms."

Honor shook her head and pulled away. She needed to put some distance between the two of them. It was clear that even after eight years apart her feelings toward him had never changed.

"I'm late for meeting with my aunt. I can clean them up there. Thank you again for pushing me out of the way, and I'm sorry I yelled at you."

He lowered his brows and put his fists on his hips. "Don't thank me and don't apologize, but are you sure you're okay to be driving?"

She nodded. "I'm fine. I don't want my aunt to worry, but I need to go. I'll help you clean up everything when I get back, Connie."

Connie shook her head. "No, dear, I'll get it. You just be careful." The other woman hugged her then went into the inn, presumably to get something to clean the mess.

"It will get cleaned. Go, Honor," Jackson said. "If you're too busy to take care of yourself, then you're too busy to take care of others. Drive safe to your aunt's." He turned then, his hands still fisted as if he were angry or... maybe as though he were trying to hold himself back from touching her.

The latter seemed like her own imagination though since he was Jackson and didn't need her.

He never had.

Leaving Jackson on the sidewalk, Honor got into her car without a backward glance and made her way to her aunt's place. She'd been to Holiday countless times as a child to visit, but hadn't been back for eight years. The last visit had been when she'd been finishing graduate school and wanted a break. Her aunt's warm home, filled with flowers and the scent of lemon oil, always made her feel as though she could stay forever and escape her problems.

Not that escaping her problems had helped in the past, but now she was here to face them head-on.

On that last visit, she'd met Jackson. Yes, during all her other visits, she'd known about the sexy Cooper brothers and had sighed and swooned with the rest of the female population, but that last visit was where she'd been more than a sideline.

She'd been twenty-five, he thirty, and they'd had the best summer she could have imagined. They'd dated and slept together. Even though it was a summer romance, they had been old enough to know the consequences of what they were doing and had set barriers in place so, when she left, it wouldn't hurt to do so.

God, she'd been an idiot.

She'd fallen in love with him and had told him so, saying she'd stay in Holiday and work there doing something else without her graduate degree so he could keep his new practice.

Hell, she'd about died when she'd said that to him.

Honor parked in her aunt's driveway and closed her eyes.

His whole face had closed off, and he'd pushed her away, telling her to grow up and leave so she could fulfill her dreams. She might have walked away, but he'd pushed her first.

Though it had hurt like hell, now she knew he'd done it for her own good. If he hadn't been cruel—whether he'd meant it or not—she'd have stayed and ruined her chances

31

at her career. She might have even resented him for letting her give up her life for him.

He hadn't even introduced her to his brothers when they'd been together. She should have known it had only been for the summer like they'd planned and not for a lifetime like she'd hoped.

At twenty-five, she'd been a young idiot. Now, at thirty-three, she was ready to learn from her mistakes and get on with her life and her duties—without Jackson.

Her heart did that annoying shudder in her chest, and she shook her head.

Nope. She didn't need Jackson, and her damn heart would just have to get over him like she'd been doing for almost a decade.

Honor made her way through her aunt's front door and ran a hand through her hair, wincing as she remembered belatedly that she needed to clean the cuts and scrapes from sliding across the sidewalk when Jackson has pushed her to the ground.

She held back a shudder at the thought. Sadly, it wasn't the almost dying that made her want to wrap her arms around herself. No, it was the memory of Jackson's warm weight along her body as he protected her.

Damn man.

"What the hell happened to you, girl?" her aunt Clementine said as she strode into the foyer, her bright red hair in a uniquely coiffed hairstyle.

There was nothing usual about her aunt. The woman screamed unique. With the bright Crayola-red hair, the not-overdone but blatant makeup and form-fitting outfits, her aunt looked as though she should be in Vegas, not in a small town in Montana.

No one really understood Clementine, and that's how Honor liked it. The woman was herself no matter the cost, and people seemed to respect her for it—even if they didn't say it.

"I fell," Honor said simply as she walked into the kitchen, Clementine on her heels clucking like a mother hen.

"Sit down at the table, and I'll take care of your cuts," her aunt ordered, and Honor obeyed.

Really, there wasn't a point in not doing what her aunt said.

"It wasn't that big a deal." Liar. "I was walking out of the inn, and a flowerpot fell from a window above me." She paused for a split second. "Someone pushed me out of the way, and I hit the sidewalk. Hence the cuts and scrapes."

Clementine raised a brow at her hesitation on the word someone but cleaned out her wounds without a word, as if she were trying to find a diplomatic way to say what needed to be said.

Okay, diplomatic probably wasn't the right word considering the type of woman her aunt was, but at least Clementine was trying.

"You could have been killed, Honor," her aunt said as she finished up.

Honor repressed that annoying shudder and shook her head. "I was fine."

"Yes, because someone saved you. I wonder who that could be."

Honor rolled her eyes. "You're the Ivory Queen, not a witch or a mind reader."

Clementine raised her chin. "Oh, we'll discuss my being the Ivory Queen in a moment, dear niece, but first I want to know what you think about that very handsome dentist."

Honor rubbed her temples. Dear Lord, she never could get anything past her aunt no matter how hard she tried.

"Jackson is just a...well; he isn't a friend, is he? He's just there. What happened was a long time ago, and we're both over it."

Liar.

Wow, she was doing great at lying to herself today.

Her aunt waited for more then let out a sigh. "If that's the way you want to play it, then fine, Honor. It's going to come back and bite you in the ass, but whatever."

Honor snorted. "You know, most aunts don't curse like a sailor in front of their nieces."

Clementine raised a brow. "Well, most aunts don't have to deal with the politics and duties of reining in thousands of tooth fairies. As it is, I'm tired, and we're going to need to open a new warehouse soon so we can store all those baby teeth."

Honor frowned at her aunt's words. Clementine had never once said she was tired or sick or anything other than strong and vital. She looked at her aunt's face and noticed a few wrinkles around her eyes that hadn't been there before.

"I'm sorry I was gone so long."

Clementine gave a sad smile. "You left because your heart was broken. I understand, dear. Yes, you could have started your duties as a tooth fairy earlier, but you're here now. We managed just find without you, though I'm glad you're here."

"I left you having to find another person to watch over the territory assigned to me. That can't be forgiven so easily."

Her aunt shook her head and poured them glasses of water with strawberries and mint—nothing too acidic for their teeth. "Brent took care of your territory just fine. Honestly, we don't even need two fairies so close to each other since he handled the work easily, but we like another person in Holiday because that's where the Ivory Queen always resides. Or at least, has since Holiday was founded."

"Well, I'm back, but I don't want to step on any toes, you know?"

Her aunt smiled and took a sip of her

water. "You won't. Brent was fine when I told him you were returning. Honestly, now he'll have more time to move on with his life and live normally."

"Wait, has he been neglecting his own happiness because he had to do my work?" Shame filled her again, and she set down her glass.

"Shut up. You needed time to grow up and find something you love to do besides teeth. I get that, Honor. Fairies usually don't start working until their mid-thirties anyway— that way they have time to live their lives normally before they do things magically. You were only starting early because of who I am, not because you necessarily wanted to."

"I'd made a promise though, and I broke it."

Her aunt clucked her tongue again and took another sip. "You left so you could grow up and nurse a broken heart. If you'd stayed— even after Jackson—you'd have resented everyone for it, and that wouldn't make a good tooth fairy, would it?"

Honor shook her head.

"That's right. Fairies need to love what

they do because like Christmas, Easter, and all the other holidays children love, they need the tooth fairy to show them that their dreams and hopes can come true. We're the ones who show that bit of magic and take their teeth—and a copy of their favorite memories—with us. We leave a coin... well, more these days because of inflation, to show the children that people are thinking of them. We then implant the memories in their parents' minds to let them think they're the ones doing it, hence bringing them closer to their children."

Honor smiled as her aunt went through the reasons her kind existed. "I love you, Aunt Clementine."

Her aunt snorted and turned her head, but not before Honor caught the misty look in her eyes.

"You're back now, and you get to relearn how to make children's dreams come true. I know you have other plans with the camp you're setting up with the town, and I'll be there to help if you need it. Don't let your past and fears ruin what you could have, Honor."

Honor stood up and hugged her aunt, not surprised when Clementine hugged her hard right back. Her aunt might act gruff and curse like a sailor, but she was still her flesh and blood.

Speaking of....

She pulled back and sighed. "Tucker's pissed, by the way."

At the mention of Honor's brother, Clementine laughed. "That boy is an idiot. I love him, don't get me wrong, but he's an idiot."

"He didn't want me to come back. It took all I had to stop him from coming here and kicking Jackson's ass when I left. Thank you for that."

Clementine rolled her eyes. "Tuck needed to know why you were leaving in such a hurry. Big brothers need to protect their sisters, even if it annoys them. It's in their blood."

"Well, I practically had to tie him down. Now he's pissed because he thinks I'm coming here to get back with Jackson. Yeah, like I'd prostrate myself, begging for scraps. No, thank you. That's over. Oh, and Tuck's mad that I'm joining the family business. He might know about magic, but he doesn't like it."

Much like someone else she knew.

Not that he'd ever told her that, but Clementine had mentioned it.

Clementine sighed and poured herself some more water. "I don't know where I went wrong with that boy."

"Considering he was raised by our straight-laced, magic-hating parents, I have an idea," Honor said wryly.

"At least you came out okay," Clementine said with a smile. "And don't worry about Tucker. I'm sure he'll turn around."

Honor grinned. "I keep telling you that you're not a mind reader or witch, yet you keep acting like one."

Her aunt fluffed out her too-red hair. "What can I say? It's a gift."

Honor snorted and brought her aunt into another hug. She'd needed this. She'd needed to come home to Holiday, even if Jackson didn't want her there. She had a job to do—two in fact—and she couldn't wait to get started.

Hiding from the eldest Cooper brother,

however, might make things a bit difficult.

Good thing Honor was up for a challenge.

CHAPTER 3

Jackson poured the rich brew down his throat and closed his eyes, savoring the taste. He might act like a clean-cut business man, but hell, a good beer seemed to make anything better after a long-ass day.

Since he'd spent the past two days trying not to think about a certain woman, he thought he deserved a beer or three.

Springsteen belted from the speakers as people played pool in the back under dim lighting. Others sat at the bar, either alone with their drink or talking about whatever was on their mind.

The Cooper brothers sat in their booth in the back corner of their local dive, Eddie's, each with a beer in front of him. They didn't get out as much as they liked, but Jackson was glad they got the chance tonight.

"Do you remember when we used to do shots on these nights?" Justin asked, his eyes closed as he leaned his head against the back of the booth. "I know we don't do whiskey anymore because a certain brother of ours had an incident."

Jackson held back a shudder as his stomach threatened to revolt at just the memory of that night of the whiskey shots. Thank God he wasn't that guy anymore.

"We're too old for that shit," Tyler said as he rubbed the back of his neck. "I might not be as old as some of you, but hell, Abigail is ten damn years younger than me."

Matt chuckled. "Can't keep up with her, old man?" At thirty, Matt was the youngest of the Cooper brothers and made sure everyone knew it.

Considering they'd tormented the bastard growing up because he was the youngest, Jackson guessed it was fair Matt was taking it out on them now.

Tyler punched Matt's shoulder then took a sip of his beer. "Fuck you. None of us are in our twenties anymore, but hell, we're not old."

Jackson nodded, though he didn't quite believe it. "I have two years until I hit the big four-zero and I already have gray at my temples. I think I've already hit old."

Brayden shook his head, his too-long hair brushing his forehead. "You're only as old as you feel. We might all be tired right now because of our pregnant wives—and my three kids—but we've still got some steam."

Jackson raised his brow. "And what's my excuse?"

Justin grinned and grabbed a handful of peanuts. "You're just an ass from what I hear along the Holiday grapevine. Guess that adds fatigue."

Jackson closed his eyes and held back a sigh. "The grocery store?"

"Yep," Matt said, and Jackson could tell the bastard was smiling. "You are an ass, but only to those who deserve it, like Jessica. You're just broody to everyone else."

Jackson opened his eyes as Tyler smiled.

"You know broody is in right now," his sheriff brother said with a grin. "Just get some vampire teeth or shift into a wolf and any woman would have you."

Jackson growled, and Tyler nodded again. "Yep, Jacks, growl just like that for the ladies, and they'll come right to you."

His brothers laughed, and Jackson was forced to join in or be left out. "Wait, do those really exist?" he asked, despite himself.

Justin shook his head. Since he worked for Santa—of all people—and Mr. Kringle was the undecided head of all things holiday magical, it made sense that Justin would know.

"The big man said only holiday magics. Well, holiday as in something that is significant to others that happens yearly or daily. No shifters or vamps. Yeah, I guess they could go with Halloween, but I guess that's why we have ghosts and witches." He elbowed Matt, who sighed.

"Thank God I'm not a ghost anymore," his youngest brother grumbled, and Jackson agreed. Though he hadn't known Matt had been a ghost the entire time he'd been noncorporeal, it still haunted him that his family had been in jeopardy. He'd never seen his brother as a ghost until the night Matt had saved Jordan's life. It still surprised him that he hadn't known.

"Magic isn't that bad," Brayden said as he leaned back. "I might have given mine to Allison, but our kids are half-gnome, so it's always going to be there."

"True, but your luck helped you," Matt said. "I was literally shackled to a house on certain nights."

Jackson sipped his beer and listened as the rest of his brothers chimed in with their new powers. Tyler, as a cupid, could feel when someone was near another who would be their soul mate. Justin, as Santa's executive, used magic along with his wife, an elf, to help the children of Holiday find their happiness.

Jackson had none of that.

Thank God.

"There's got to be something about this town and us though."

Jackson blinked at Tyler's words. "What's that?"

Tyler narrowed his eyes. "Thanks for paying attention. What I was saying is that we all know Holiday is the mecca, but we don't know why. We don't even know who knows what and what else might exist in town. We also don't know why we Coopers seem to be drawn to it and we're immune to the gnomes' magic."

Jackson shrugged. "Does it matter?"

Brayden frowned. "You're the one who always likes to look for answers. It's why you liked science so much in school. You're honestly telling us you don't care about why things are the way they are?"

"No, I don't. I'm not magical, and I'm happy that way. I'm not about to poke the hornet's nest and end up like Abigail with new powers that I can't control."

Tyler snarled, but Matt held him back.

"Leave my wife out of this. She's learning to be a harpy."

"Yeah? She'll always have to deal with the fact she has a temper she can't control and can't eat off her own plate. What about your kids? Or any of your kids? Why would you want to subject yourselves to that?"

Brayden shook his head. "We can't change the way things are, but we can figure out why they are. That might help with control. As for our kids? They're going to be loved and cared for, no matter what, so back the fuck off."

Jackson winced. "Hell, I'm sorry. I didn't mean anything like that. You know I'm going to love those babies like they're my own. I'm already Uncle Jacks, and I'm going to love all the babies that come into your lives.

His brothers nodded, their tempers soothed a bit.

Jessica had been right; he was an ass.

"I'm off my game, sorry," he said as he drained his glass and asked for a round of waters. Since they all were going to different places afterward, they didn't have a designated driver, hence the one-beer limit.

"I have a feeling why you're so jumpy," Matt said as he smiled.

Dread filled him, and he fought to keep his expression remote. "Yes?"

"Really? What happened?" Brayden asked with a grin on his face.

Jackson looked at Justin's and Tyler's smiles and wanted to leave Eddie's right then. Apparently the damn Holiday grapevine had struck again. Since all Cooper women were pregnant with mini Coopers, the only gossip left was for Jackson.

Hell.

"It seems there's a new town resident," Brayden drawled, and Jackson eyed the door.

So. Far. Away.

"Ah yes, the raven-haired goddess, according to town gossip," Matt said with a laugh.

"Don't let Jordan hear you say that," Jackson bit out.

The description of Honor did fit, but he wasn't going to mention that.

"Who do you think told me?" Matt explained. "Now where was I? Oh yes, this new girl seems to know you. So well in fact that she stopped by your clinic and had a tense conversation in front of your receptionist, Veronica."

Damn Veronica.

"Not to mention that you later saved Honor's life when you threw your body on top of hers," Tyler said with a smile.

"I hear he practically made sweet, sweet love to her while he was on the ground," Justin added in.

"Sweet, sweet love?" Jackson said, holding back a smile. Hell, the gossips were having a party with this.

"Yes, sweet, sweet love," Brayden agreed.

"There was no loving, sweet or otherwise, going on," Jackson explained. "I just pushed her out of the way so the damn flowerpot wouldn't hit her."

All four men stared at him with knowing expressions.

"I repeat. No loving."

The image of Honor naked as she rode him from above, her full breasts bouncing along with her fast rhythm, filled his mind.

Well, fuck.

"Sure," Matt drawled. "That doesn't tell us much though. How do you know this goddess?"

Jackson let out a sigh. There really was no getting out of this. He could either deal with his brothers now or be forced to answer the endless questions from their wives later.

He held back a shudder.

Anything but that.

"I knew her when she came to visit her aunt before. That's it."

Tyler furrowed his brows. "She's Clementine's niece, right? Honor Bridges?"

Jackson nodded and drained his water glass, suddenly very thirsty. He signaled for another one and winced. He'd have to piss like a racehorse soon if he kept this up.

"That can't be it," Brayden put in. "I mean, if you're acting all broody over her and had that intense chat in your office, it has to be something more."

"Fine," Jackson bit out. "We dated over a summer years ago when she visited her aunt. She left. I stayed. No big deal."

His brothers were silent for a moment, and he cursed himself. He shouldn't have added that last part. It had been a big fucking deal, but they didn't have to know about it.

"You dated her for a whole summer, and we didn't know?" Tyler asked. "When was this?"

"Eight years ago. What does it matter?"

"Eight years ago you were thirty. This wasn't some teenage lovesick thing, Jacks," Brayden said softly.

"No, it wasn't. It was just a fun time for a summer. It was over, and it's still over. Don't make a big thing about it."

Justin stared at him, concern in his gaze. "Why didn't you tell us about her when you were dating?"

Jackson held back a wince. He hadn't told them because he'd like Honor too much, but they couldn't know that. Hell, he didn't want to get into that now, or ever for that matter.

"It wasn't a bit deal then, and it's even less of one now. Just drop it, guys."

Matt shook his head. "I don't think we can. The women have all got it in their heads that Honor means something to you, or at least she did. You know what that means, right?"

Jackson cursed. "They need to stop fucking matchmaking. I know you're all happy with what you have, and fuck, I'm happy for you, but I like being alone. Okay? I don't want a wife. I don't want kids. I don't want magic. I just want to live like I'm living now, and I don't want to change that. My relationship with Honor is over. I'm not going to be with her again and just because she moved back to town doesn't mean I'm going to act like Matt did over Jordan and get with her again. Got it?"

Liar.

"You're denying it all a little quickly, don't you think?" Matt said with a grin.

"Fuck you. I don't love Honor. I didn't before." Liar. "It's not the same as you and Jordan. Get it through your thick skulls, okay? Honor moved back to be with her aunt, not to see me. She only met with me in my office out of courtesy. Though, really, she hadn't even needed to do that."

Tyler shook his head. "You sure are getting riled up over a woman you say you're over."

Jackson closed his eyes and took a deep breath. Shit. If he kept denying it, they'd think he was just denying his feelings. If he didn't deny it, they'd think he wanted Honor.

There really wasn't any way to deal with this other than kick the shit out of them like he had for years...or at least try.

Tyler narrowed his eyes, his cop face on. "Don't even think about. I'm not about to get kicked out of Eddie's because you're in a fucking mood. I'm the sheriff for God's sake. Now I got this new deputy, Hugh, and I need to act like I run this town, not like I brawl."

"I wasn't going to hit you," Jackson lied. "Though, if I did, you'd just have to deal with being known as the pansy ass who got his butt kicked by his older brother."

Tyler scoffed. "Really? That's how you're going to play it?"

"Settle down now, boys," Brayden intervened. "Jacks, don't rile him up just because you don't want to talk about your lady love."

"She's not my damn lady love," Jackson spat.

"I'll remind you that you said that when you're married and you have all those babies you're afraid of," Justin said.

Jackson threw up his hands. "I give up. You guys think what you want, but know this, I am not with Honor Bridges, nor will I ever be. Got it?"

He pushed Matt out of the booth, got up and walked out the door ignoring Tyler's parting remark.

"Famous last words, bro."

Fuck.

He cursed himself for letting his brothers see below the surface as he made his way home and jumped in the shower to get the bar smell off of him before he went to bed.

Jackson turned the water up as hot as he could take and let the spray beat down on him. His shoulders were knotted, his back aching like an old man's, and all he wanted to do was sleep like someone far older than he was.

He hadn't been lying to his brothers when he'd said he'd wanted to be alone in his life. The only time he'd ever thought about a future with someone had been with Honor, not that he'd ever admit that to anyone.

Now that Honor was back, though, yeah, the ideas that kept popping in his head were going to be hard as hell to get over.

He didn't like these thoughts of futures and babies and sweet, sweet love.

Fuck, now he sounded like some love-lost idiot.

The image of Honor's wide blue eyes and sexy little smile flashed across his mind, and he groaned. His hand ran down his chest along the rivulets of water and wrapped around his cock before he even thought about what he was doing.

It had been way too long since he'd had a woman, and now all he could think about was filling Honor's warm pussy or that delectable mouth of hers. She'd loved it when he'd have her kneel in front of him, her hair wrapped tightly around his fist as he fucked her mouth.

Jackson pumped his hips as he fucked his fist, a little drop of cum pearling at the head of his cock. He imagined Honor's lips around his cock, her gentle hands rolling his balls as she swallowed him fully. He'd run his hand down her chest, cupping her breasts and rolling her nipples between his fingers, loving the way her eyes would darken as he pinched hard.

He grunted her name as he came, his seed covering the shower wall and his chest. The water washed it away, and Jackson groaned.

Seriously?

He'd just come like a teenager thinking about a girl.

He'd thought he'd grown past that, but apparently he'd been mistaken.

He quickly soaped himself and cleaned up before turning off the showerhead. Images of Honor beneath him and then against the wall filled his mind as he dried off, not bothering to put on pajamas. His cock filled again, and he got into bed, pointedly ignoring the damn thing.

Weren't men his age supposed to deal with fewer erections? Okay fine, he wasn't that old, but seriously, this was getting ridiculous. Why was it that with one thought of Honor, he was back to being a teen who couldn't keep it down?

He fell asleep with her on his mind, but

he just let it come. It didn't matter. It wasn't as if he could control his dreams.

Jackson dreamt of himself standing above his body in his bedroom, this time wearing at least pants.

What the hell?

He could tell it was a dream because everything was a little hazy, but it felt really fucking real to him.

"I see you know you're sleeping," a voice said from behind him.

Jackson whirled around, his heart beating against his chest in a fast staccato. "Who the hell are you?"

This was one weird fucking nightmare.

The man standing before him wore jeans and a T-shirt. His brown eyes, brown hair, and everything else about him looked so average Jackson wasn't sure if he'd even remember the man later.

"I'm a friend of a friend," the stranger explained. "Do you know who the sandman is?"

Jackson blinked. "Yeah. He's the one who puts little kids to sleep. You're telling me you're him?

The stranger just smiled. "No, I'm not him, but I know him. Or at least, one of the sandmen. He owed me a favor, and now you're going to take the brunt of it."

"What do you mean? I'm going to wake up now."

He tried but couldn't, as if someone was forcing him to stay asleep.

The stranger laughed. "I'll let you wake up in a moment. First, I want to tell you about the sandman. You see, it is said that they sprinkle sand or dust on or into the eyes of a child at night to bring on dreams or sleep. The grit or blinking when they wake up is the result of the sandman's work."

Considering all Jackson had seen within his family, it didn't surprise him that the sandman existed, but hell, this guy was freaking him out.

"Okay, yeah, I knew the stories, but why are you telling me about them?"

The stranger grinned. "I wanted you to know your new job."

"What? Oh fuck no. I'm not a sandman."

"No, but you will be. You see, I know you hate magic, so what better way to punish someone than to make them deal with what they hate?"

The stranger moved to stand over Jackson's sleeping body, and Jackson reached out to grab him, only to come up with air.

"You're asleep, dumb-ass. You can't touch anyone unless you have the powers of the sand."

"What the hell did I ever do to you? Why are you doing this?"

The stranger took out a pouch and poured black sand into his palm. "Oh, it's not you, but don't worry, it'll still hurt the one I want to hurt. Now, the sand you'll use in the future is gold. This black stuff is to make a new sandman."

Jackson tried to wake himself up, pinching his arms and thrashing, but nothing worked.

"Don't do this," he begged.

The stranger shook his head. "Be sure to

thank Honor for this." He sprinkled the black sand on Jackson's eyes, and in the dream, Jackson screamed, an odd power squeezing him tight as darkness threatened to take hold.

Honor?

This man wanted to hurt Honor. That couldn't happen, but hell, how was he going to stop it?

Jackson's vision blurred as he fell to his knees, an odd sense of something far greater than him taking over. His arms shook, his body broke out in a sweat. Magic—it had to be magic—filled him.

He didn't want to be the sandman.

He didn't want this magic.

He didn't want anything.

CHAPTER 4

Honor had to be dreaming—there wasn't another answer for it. She stood in the field next to the lake she loved so much, yet everything felt a bit off. It was as if she were walking through fog, trying to get to the other side of the lake but couldn't.

Why would she be dreaming about this lake?

"Honor, you're here," Jackson said.

Honor turned to him, her heart in her throat. "Jackson," she croaked.

Great, now she was dreaming about the

man.

Again.

"I don't know why you're here or why I'm dreaming about you, but I'm so glad you're here." He walked toward her then framed her face with his large hands. "God, I missed you. I can't tell you that when I'm awake, but I do. I think everything is about to go crazy, but thank God you're here."

Honor blinked. Something was wrong. This might have been a dream, but it felt a little too real for her.

"Jackson, I don't think—"

The alarm woke her up and she blinked as her eyes opened.

That was weird.

Really freaking weird.

She got out of bed and started getting ready for the day, but Jackson was never far from her thoughts. In reality though, he'd never left her thoughts for long in all this time.

The knock on the door surprised Honor. She wasn't expecting anyone, and considering she didn't know anyone in Holiday other than

Jackson, Clementine, and Connie, Honor had no idea who it could be. Yes, she'd visited Holiday several times before, but she'd only stayed with her aunt and met with Jackson. She'd been too shy to really meet others before.

Connie was out of town for the next week, leaving Honor with free range of the inn. Her aunt would have just walked in, closed door be damned. And there was no way Jackson would be stopping by so...

Since there was no peep hole, she opened the door and froze.

"Jackson?"

Dear Lord, the man looked as though he hadn't slept. Instead of his normal slacks and buttoned shirt, he wore a plain white T-shirt and old, faded jeans that encased his thighs quite nicely.

She tore her gaze upward to his unshaven face and pulled him into her bedroom, closing the door behind him.

"What's wrong? What happened?"

He shook his head then opened his mouth to speak; only nothing came out.

"Come sit down, Jacks, and tell me what happened. Is it your brothers? Their wives? I heard they were all pregnant. Is everyone okay?"

He looked so lost, as though someone had pulled the rug right out from under him. She'd never seen him this way. He'd always been so cool and collected, except when he'd been younger and she'd broken through his shields. He'd laughed with her in the privacy of their summer, but this was different.

She forced him to sit on the edge of the bed then ran her hands through his hair like he'd loved when they'd been together. He'd cut it short, but she could still get a good handful if she wanted.

"They're fine. It's not about them," he said, his voice a little hollow.

Honor cupped his cheeks, ignoring the way his stubble scraped against her skin, causing her to remember other places his beard had done just that when they'd been together.

Damn it, this wasn't the time to skip down memory lane.

"What is it, Jacks? You're scaring me."

He tilted his head up, and she looked into those deep blue eyes, her heart racing.

"I think I'm scaring myself."

She rubbed her thumb along his cheek, letting him take his time.

"I had a visitor last night," he said, his voice gruff.

Honor resisted the urge to grind her teeth at that thought. A visitor? As in a woman he slept with? There really wasn't any reason she needed to know that or imagine the perky boob model spreading her legs for him.

Okay, that was a little too jealous for her.

"Okay," she said.

"I don't know why I came here, Honor. I mean, you don't know about Holiday and what happens here, so now I'm just sitting here and going to make you think I'm crazy. God, maybe I am crazy."

His behavior made her stand straighter. Oh, she might not know the day-to-day things in Holiday, but she knew enough about the secret goings-on—including the fact that the

Coopers seemed to be attracted to magic.

The brothers couldn't hide that from her aunt after all.

"Jackson, are you talking about magic?" she asking, bracing herself for an outburst.

His eyes widened, and then he clenched his jaw. "So you know?"

She nodded then brushed his cheek again, needing to touch him, even though she knew it was a mistake. "Yes, Jackson, I know. My aunt's told me all about you Cooper brothers and everything that's gone on."

He swallowed hard, and she marveled how sexy he looked as his throat worked.

Damn, so not the time.

"I knew most of the town knew about Jordan being a witch, even though they don't really believe it, but I didn't know they knew about everything else."

Honor shook her head. "I don't think everyone knows, but my aunt does."

She took a deep breath, preparing herself for the inevitable outcome when she told him the truth. It wasn't as if they'd ever had a chance anyway.

"Why would your aunt know about us?"

"Tell me what happened last night, Jacks," she said, hedging away from the question.

"I will once you tell me what you're hiding." His voice held a slight edge, but she ignored it. He was usually all bluster—or so she'd remembered.

Honor blew out a breath then shrugged, pulling her hands from his face. The loss of contact annoyed her, but she needed to get over it.

"Fine. My aunt is the Ivory Queen. Meaning she's the queen of all tooth fairies. I'm also a tooth fairy, though I haven't been doing my duty for a bit." Not like she'd tell him for how long and why. "So, yes, I get the whole magic thing and the fact that we're not as alone as we think in terms of holiday paranormals."

Jackson blinked then narrowed his eyes.

Great, here it comes.

"You're...you're one of them?"

Well, that got her back up. "Really? 'One

of them'? Prejudiced much? Aren't your brothers deeply entrenched in all of this?"

Jackson held up his hands, his color looking a little better than it had when he'd first walked in. "I'm sorry. That came out wrong. I seem to be putting my foot in my mouth more than usual lately."

Honor crossed her arms over her chest, ignoring the way Jackson's gaze went to her breasts before moving to her face.

Subtle.

"I get you're freaking out, and, yes, it wasn't something you were expecting, but you need to make sure you don't act like you're better than your brothers because you aren't magical."

Jackson winced then lay back on the bed, his shirt riding up a bit so she could see his flat stomach and that little happy trail that led to even more delicious things.

Hell, she really needed to get her mind out of the gutter.

"Why did you just wince? What's wrong?"

Jackson put his arm over his eyes and sighed. "When I can think, we'll talk about what it means that you're the tooth fairy, okay? I promise I'll sit and listen to it all and try not to act like the ass I am."

"You're not an ass." Well, not usually.

He let out a dry chuckle. "Sure, Honor, whatever you say. The reason I winced before is that when you said I wasn't magical... that isn't entirely true anymore."

Chills ran down her back, and she moved to kneel on the bed by his side, ignoring the heat that radiated off him. She moved his arm and looked down at him, not liking the frown on his face.

He reached out and held a piece of her hair in between his fingers, not really focusing on anything.

"Jackson?"

"My visitor last night knew the sandman. I don't know who the guy was, but he...hell, Honor..."

She gave into her impulses and cupped his cheek again. "Tell me."

"He threw this black dust into my eyes. Only it wasn't my eyes. I mean it was, just... hell, I'm screwing this up. I was asleep, and then I felt like I was outside my body. I watched as this guy threw black sand in my eyes and told me I'd be a sandman." He met her gaze, and she wanted to weep for him. God, he looked so scared. "I thought it was a dream, Honor. It had to be, but then it hurt, and I woke up. I had black sand in my eyes and I wiped it away like you do when you rub sleep out of your eyes. What am I going to do?"

Her stomach clenched, but she tried to hide her fear and whatever else she felt from her expression. "He made you a sandman?"

Jackson nodded. "That's what he said."

"They aren't supposed to be able to do that unless you agree, Jackson. It's against their laws."

He gave a wry smile. "I don't think the man cared. And, anyway, he said he wasn't a sandman himself, just someone who knew one."

"Oh, Jackson. I...I'm sorry."

What else could she say? It didn't make sense, yet she could feel something different about him, as if she could see something familiar...a new magic that hadn't been there before.

"I don't know what to do, Honor."

He looked so lost, so unlike the man she'd known.

Something else about what happened bugged her. "Jackson, why did you come to me with this? Before this morning, you didn't know I knew about magic or that I was magic."

He met her gaze, and she sucked in a breath. "He said to thank you, Honor. He knew who you were and said he couldn't hurt you the way he wanted, and this would have to do. What did he mean by that?"

She froze, her heart in her throat. "Why? Why would he say that? Why would they use you to hurt me? What did I do that this man, whoever he is, hates me so much?"

God, this was all her fault. Jackson was lost and immersed in something he hated because of her. She never should have come back.

He sat up abruptly and cupped her face. "Stop it. This man, whoever he is, is to blame. I don't know why he thought to hurt you through me, or why he wants to hurt you in the first place, but we're going to figure this out."

She smiled at him. "I thought you came here for answers to at least feel better. Now look at you. You're calming me down."

A shiver ran through her as the rough pad of this thumb brushed along her cheek. "I came here because he said your name. I have no fucking clue what to do now, but this isn't your fault, Honor. It's the fault of some man who wants to hurt you. He's the one to blame. We're going to figure this out."

"We will. I'll talk to my aunt, and you and I can get together to figure out how to deal with what you are now."

He sighed, and she leaned into him. "I'm sorry, Jacks. I know you don't want this, but I don't think there's a way to go back."

"I don't think so either. Hell, I've spent the past few months saying how much I hate magic, and now look at me. Karma's a bitch."

She inwardly winced at his words, but she wouldn't let him know how much they hurt her. He might hate magic, but now there was no turning back.

"Jackson…"

"No, don't worry about that. We need to talk, Honor, but I have to get to work." He ran his hand through his hair. "Damn it. I'm late. I'm never late. Can you come for dinner at my place tonight?"

Honor bit her lip then shook her head. "I'd rather not…"

Damn it. That revealed too much, but, hell, she couldn't go to his place and be alone with him.

He gave a small smile. "I know what you mean. Okay, we can go to the diner. As long as we sit in the back booth, we can talk about anything. That's how my brothers and I have always done it."

"Won't people talk?"

He gripped her chin and moved her closer so their faces almost touched. She felt his breath along her skin, and she repressed a shudder.

"They already are."

He moved away, leaving her cold, and she closed her eyes. "Fine. I'll meet you at six at the diner. I don't really care what they have to say about us as long as you don't. I might be trying to make this place my home, but I can't stop people from gossiping."

Jackson slid his fingers through her hair one more time before getting off the bed. Even as he moved, she watched the layer of ice he wore over himself like a shield taking hold.

"I'll see you at six."

With that, he left, not even looking back.

The man confused her even more than she confused herself.

She quickly finished getting ready and left the inn, hunger gnawing at her. With Connie gone, she'd had to fend for herself in terms of food, and since she'd been known to burn water, she refrained from going into the kitchen. Even the casseroles and other goodies in the freezer required too much of a chance that she'd burn the whole damn inn to the ground.

She made her way to the diner, ignoring the curious glances at the "new girl in town". Yes, she'd be going to the diner for dinner later that night, but she was hungry, and Holiday was such a small town, it didn't leave her many options.

Hell, she needed to find a place to live soon. Yes, she could have lived with her aunt, but she knew her aunt liked her own space and had a routine. She was already on the lookout for houses to buy rather than rent. She was in her thirties now, and it was time to settle down, not go from home to home until something fit.

The bell over the door rang as she walked in the diner. Considering it was after the morning rush, the place was pretty empty except for the booth in the back where the Cooper women sat talking.

Oh great, just what she needed.

"Hey!" one of the women said as she waved. "You're Honor, right? Come sit with us."

Honor stood in the center of the diner, knowing she couldn't really say no and sit alone. Well, these people were close to Jackson, so she should get to know them.

No, wait, she didn't want Jackson, so there wouldn't be a point in getting to know them.

Denial was seriously making her crazy.

Honor pasted on a smile and made her way to the four Cooper wives that she knew from sight, but not anymore than that. Aunt Clementine had been thorough in telling her about the town and who had moved in— pictures included.

"I'm Jordan, by the way," the woman who'd called her said. She was beautiful with long dark brown hair and bright eyes. Honor also knew she was a witch—a freaking strong witch. "Since we know you know Jackson, we're not going to beat around the bush and pretend you don't know why we want you to sit with us." She smiled, and Honor had to laugh.

"I think I like you already."

Honor pulled a chair over to the booth as Jordan introduced the rest of the party. "This is Rina." Jordan gestured to the smallest woman at the table with blond hair. "She's married to Justin. Oh, yeah, I'm married to Matt. Let's see, that's Abby sitting by Rina over there." She pointed to a pretty brunette with a huge smile. "And this lovely lady by me is Allison, Brayden's wife."

Honor nodded to each of them and noticed that they each had little baby bumps— though Allison's seemed to be larger than the rest.

"Yes, I know. I'm a whale."

Honor looked up at Allison and blushed. "I'm sorry. I didn't mean to stare. I had just heard that you were all about the same time along. I guess I was wrong. Oh, wait. I didn't mean you were big or anything. Well, hell, I'm just going to eat the foot in my mouth for breakfast rather than ordering. I'm so sorry."

Allison laughed while the other ladies joined her. "Don't feel bad. I didn't mean to sound bitchy." She looked over her shoulder, and Honor noticed that no one else was around. "I'm the only one having twins, so, yeah, I'm a bit bigger. I don't think I can hide it much longer."

"Twins!" Honor said quietly. "That's awesome. Wait, didn't I hear you had three kids already?"

Allison closed her eyes. "Yes. Brayden is walking around now with his chest out like he's the most virile man in the world, but yes, this will make five total."

"Wow, congrats, all of you. Jackson hadn't mentioned you were pregnant with twins —or that you were even pregnant, but yay." Belatedly, she realized she'd mentioned his name when she'd wanted to veer away from that topic of conversation for as long as possible and closed her eyes.

"Ha!" Allison laughed. "You mentioned him first, so now we get to grill you."

"We won't really grill you," Abby said. "Oh, well, we might, but we'll be gentle."

"It'll only hurt a bit," Rina chimed in.

"I'm scared. Honestly, like really, really scared right now," Honor said with a laugh.

"Don't be," Jordan said. "As for why Jackson didn't mention it, well, Allison and Brayden just told everyone this morning, and Jackson had something else on his mind. So before we grill you on your past with him— which we will—what do you know about this whole sandman thing?"

That right there was the reason Jordan was the take-charge one of the group according to her aunt. Family safety before anything else, and Honor was glad Jackson had her.

"I have no idea, you guys. Jackson showed up at my room this morning and told me about it. I guess he told you guys before he headed over then?"

Allison nodded. "We'd done a video conference call to announce it before work because I couldn't hold it in anymore, and he didn't look like himself. His brothers got it out of him, and now we're all freaking out a bit. He told us he was on his way to tell you. I guess this whole magic thing doesn't surprise you."

"Of course it wouldn't," Rina chimed in. "You're a tooth fairy, right?"

Honor nodded. "I forget that elves are really good at detecting things like that."

Rina smiled. "Yep, we're special."

Abby's eyes widened. "Okay, after we figure out what to do about Jackson, we're going to talk about you. I don't think I've ever met a tooth fairy before."

Honor smiled, liking that, unlike when she hadn't lived in Holiday, she could be open about who and what she was. "You have if you've met my Aunt Clementine."

"Really?" Abby asked. "Well, hell, this town is even weirder than I thought. In the best possible way, of course."

"I know what you mean," Honor said. "As for Jackson, I don't know. I'm scared. Did he tell you what the man said?"

They all nodded.

"Yes, that the man who hurt Jackson wanted to hurt you," Jordan said, her eyes narrowed. "I'm a witch, you know, so I can feel if someone is up to something, and I can't feel that negativity off of you, so this other man must have a reason that we can't even fathom. I feel no guilt from you, no remorse, so I know you're not part of this—not in the wrong sense, anyway."

Ignoring the rise of anger that filled her at Jordan's remark, she nodded. "We'll figure it out. We have to. I'm going to talk to my aunt after I eat and try to see what I can do."

Rina nodded. "I'm going to look around and see what I can do as well. I might know a sandman that can help. I've never heard of one losing their powers and going back to normal— or however normal a Cooper can be—but at least he'd be able to help Jackson deal with these new powers of his."

Allison pushed Jordan out of the booth. "I'm going to go get you a drink, Honor. I also planned on just ordering specials for us. You want one?"

"I can get up and do it," Honor said. "You shouldn't be standing."

Allison rolled her eyes. "You sound like every Cooper male right now. The waitress called in sick, so our cook and owner's alone. Technically, I don't work here anymore, but I'm getting us food. Sit down and go over what you can, and we'll figure it out. Jackson's not alone, and you aren't either. No matter what happened between the two of you in the past, it will stay that way—in the past—but we'll be here as your friends, no matter what."

She walked off, leaving Honor tearing up.

"She's right you know," Abby put in. "We've adopted you."

Honor stared at these women who were closely connected to the man she desperately wanted to forget but could never let go.

It seemed things were about to change, and, frankly, Honor liked it.

CHAPTER 5

"That's the last patient of the day for you," Veronica said as she walked into the exam room, her gaze on her tablet rather than Jackson's face.

Jackson finished washing his hands then dried them off, his mind on magic, changes, and Honor, rather than what he should be doing to close up before dinner.

"Jackson? Did you hear me?"

He turned toward his receptionist and nodded. "Yes, thanks for everything today. You can go home now, and I'll close up early."

Her eyes widened then narrowed. "What's up with you today? First, you're late, and then you barely talked to anyone who came in. Sure, you're usually silent and broody, but you usually talk a bit to your patients to ease their minds when you have your hands in their mouths."

"I'm not broody."

Why the hell did he always have to explain that to people?

Veronica merely raised a brow and pursed her lips. "Sure, dear, whatever you say. Now you're telling me I can go home early, and you're going to close up the place on your own early. Are you going to tell me what's going on with you? Does this have to do with Honor?"

Jackson closed his eyes and prayed for patience. He'd told Honor that the town was already talking about them as a couple, and he hadn't been lying, but hell, he just needed a moment away from it all to think.

"Go home, Veronica."

"Fine, Jackson, but don't think you can hide from me for long." She left him alone in the exam room, and he rubbed his temples.

Hadn't it been less than twenty-four hours ago that he was magic free and able to stay away from Honor? Now he was a sandman —or whatever the hell he was since he didn't really feel different—and he was about to go on a date with Honor.

Oh, he'd said it was so they could talk about things, but really? She hadn't wanted to be alone with him for the same reason he wanted to be alone with her yet dreaded it.

They'd have their clothes off within a minute of being alone, and he'd sink his cock into her warmth as soon as he could. He'd felt the sparks when they'd both been on her bed that morning, and it had only been the tension of the events that had stopped him from kissing her.

It was hard as hell to stay away from her.

Now they were going to go out in public and eat and try to talk about what it meant to be a sandman and the tooth fairy. Too bad that probably wouldn't be happening considering that, yes, Holiday might know about some of the paranormal and his favorite booth made most things private, but he had a feeling things weren't going to go as they wanted.

This was a date.

He just needed to hop like that freaking rabbit and scream he was late for that very important date and he'd be one step further down that rabbit hole of insanity.

Jackson closed up the practice and drove to the diner, his palms clammy. He could have lied and said it was from the subject matter of their supposed talk, but, in reality, he was nervous to see her.

He was almost forty for God's sake, not a teenager. He needed to act like it.

As he walked into the diner, he could have sworn conversation stopped for a beat before picking up again. Their curious glances bore into his back and everywhere else so hard he almost wanted to look down to make sure he'd zipped up his fly.

Honor sat in the far booth with two waters on the table and a faraway expression on her face. She'd worn her hair down like he loved—not that he'd tell her that. No, he needed to keep his distance.

He had a feeling that wasn't going to happen though. Honor had been the one woman he'd seen himself having a future with, and then he'd forced her to go. Not only to make sure she lived her life and fulfilled her dreams, but because he'd gotten scared as hell.

No one else since then had made him want to forego his plans of living alone until he died, and he knew no one else would. When Honor had first come to town, he'd tried to tell himself—he still tried to tell himself—that he wouldn't do anything with her, that he'd go on without her and just deal with the fact that she lived in the same town as him.

As he watched her gaze reach his and heard his quick intake of breath, he knew he'd been an idiot to think he'd even had a chance of staying away.

Either he'd force himself to act like he didn't care, or he could maybe think of her as something more than just his past.

He didn't know, and frankly, it was up to her, but damn, he wanted her.

There, he'd said it.

He wanted Honor.

Now he just needed to figure out what he wanted to do about it.

Jackson ignored the murmurs and looks as he went to the back booth and sat across from her.

"Hi," she said, her voice a bit breathless.

Good, at least she felt something too. Or at least he hoped she did.

Hell, he needed time to think about all of this. Too much was going on at once, and for a man who liked things orderly, he was freaking out. Nothing seemed to be that way at the moment.

"Hi," he said, and they fell into an awkward silence.

What exactly could he say to an ex-girlfriend who came back into town after leaving eight years prior, who also happened to be a tooth fairy, niece of the Ivory Queen, and, in some way, connected with the man who'd turned him into a sandman?

He didn't think there was a self-help book or Hallmark card for this special occasion.

"I didn't order us anything since I don't know if you still like the same things," she said, her voice rushed. "Though, really, we never actually went out on dates so..."

He winced at the reminder he'd treated her so poorly before by hiding her from Holiday.

"Ask me anything and I'll tell you," he said.

She tilted her head and frowned. "What are we doing here, Jackson?"

"I take it you don't mean in the diner."

"No, and you knew that. What are we doing eating together when we could have done this with your family and probably gotten more information out of it?" Her eyes widened. "Unless you're still hiding me from them, and then we've got a problem because I just had breakfast with all of your sisters-in-law this morning."

Now he felt like the ass everyone called him.

There had to be a way he could fix this.

He reached out and grabbed her hand, ignoring the whispered and no-so-whispered gasps and comments from their audience.

"I don't know what we're doing, but

whatever it is, we'll figure it out together. I know things are convoluted at the moment, but it will get better. As for my family, it obviously didn't occur to me to talk with them and you because I wanted to be with just you. I'm sorry."

She blushed that pretty shade of pink he knew covered her whole body, and he shifted as his cock hardened.

"Since most of the people in town are currently staring at us, we can't talk about everything in private. I'm sorry I wanted us to be in public. I guess that didn't make much sense."

Jackson grinned, and he heard even more gasps. He knew he didn't smile much, but, hell, people really needed to mind their own business. He looked over his shoulder and glared. Everyone quickly turned away and busied themselves.

Finally.

"Since we're not going to talk about everything we need to talk about, including the tension currently between us," Jackson began, "let's talk about you. It's been eight years, Honor. What did I miss?"

"Well, I finished graduate school, and now I'm here to open up a family-friendly, eco-friendly camp." She smiled, and he blinked.

"Really? In Holiday?"

She nodded. "Yep. Aunt Clementine said Holiday was dying down because you guys needed more jobs and more men. Her words, not mine. Since my degree is in helping to direct marketing, tourism, and outdoor activities, I thought Holiday was the perfect place for me to work. The camp will bring in hotels and cabins, restaurants and more. All of those will bring in more jobs."

"You're going to bring more people into Holiday."

"Yes. I didn't know the condition of the town, but Aunt Clementine told me. I've already talked with the town council over the internet and phone calls. The plans are already made and most everything is signed. I'm just getting ready to finish the last plans before I hire people to build, design, and do other things. My job is to organize and the fact that I know about the environment helps that."

She leaned closer. "I'm also going to bring in more people like you said. Magical and non-magical. The area is beautiful, Jackson, and we're not using its beauty to bring people in safely. I want to open an environmentally friendly outdoor area where the town will thrive. This way people will come in, spend money, and leave without disrupting the town and surrounding area's ecosystem."

She smiled as she described it, and Jackson knew he was in love with the woman just like he had been before. No, he'd always loved her; he'd just tried to forget it all.

"That sounds like a big project."

"It is, but I can do it."

"I know you can."

"You always did believe in me," she said, and then she drank from her glass of her water.

"Of course, Honor. Where are you going to build this place?"

She grinned at him, and he held back a groan. That was her naughty grin. Hell. "Oh, you know the place—the lake by your place."

He closed his eyes as images of how the moonlight danced along her naked body as they skinny-dipped late at night flooded his mind. They'd made love in that lake, near that lake, and around that lake countless times.

He still remembered a time where a fish got a little too friendly...

Honor threw her head back and laughed, catching the attention of the diner again. "You're remembering the fish, aren't you?"

Jackson rested his face in his hands. "God, that damn fish."

"You always get this little line between your brows when you remember that frisky fish."

Thankfully, the waitress stopped by and took their order before he had to talk about the fish that knew a little too much about certain parts of his anatomy.

"So the lake is owned by the town and I already have the permits saying we can build on it. The town will own the camp and I'll hire people to run it. This way the money goes directly into the community, not someone's pockets."

They talked about her place in California and how she was looking for a place in Holiday now. They talked about her aunt and her crazy hair. They talked about Jackson's sisters-in-law and their addictions to peanut butter.

They talked about pretty much everything except the magic running through each of their veins and the fact that they both still wanted the other.

When the check was paid, Jackson led her out to their cars, again ignoring the pointed glances headed their way.

"Are you off tomorrow?" Honor asked as they made their way to her car. Thankfully she'd parked on the side of the building with no windows so they were alone for the first time that night.

"Yes, though I usually go in and do paperwork. I don't need to though. We can talk tomorrow about what happened and what will happen."

"You're not just talking about what happened last night, are you?"

He shook his head as he backed her to the car. Her breasts pressed against his chest, and he framed her face with his hands.

"No, I'm not just talking about what

happened when I was asleep. This connection we have? I don't understand it, but we need to do something about it."

He leaned down so his lips brushed against hers, but he didn't press harder, liking the tease and taste just as much.

"I thought you wanted nothing to do with what would come with that," she said on a breath. He felt her hand come up his back below his shirt, and he shuddered.

"Maybe I changed my mind." He licked her bottom lip and bit down softly, loving the way she gasped into his mouth.

"I don't know if I believe that, but we can talk about it tomorrow." She rocked her hips so she cradled his erection, and they both moaned.

"Tomorrow," he agreed then lowered his lips to touch hers fully.

Her lips parted, and he let his tongue dance with hers, their breaths in sync as he kissed her again after all this time. He knew they should have talked more before doing this, but he didn't care.

He couldn't care, not with her taste on

his tongue.

He pulled back, leaving them both breathless, and then tucked a lock of hair behind her ear. "I'll follow you to the inn since it's on my way home."

She nodded, her lips swollen from his kiss, her eyes a little glazed.

"Are you okay to drive?"

She smiled then looked down at his dick. "Well, if you can drive with a second stick shift, I think I can make it."

He threw his head back and laughed then let her get in her car. He ran back to his so he could follow her, shaking his head as he did so. Hell, he was crazy, but he didn't care, not when all he could smell was her crisp floral scent and he could still taste her like he'd drown in her essence. They'd probably just made a mistake and were going to make another tomorrow, but for some reason, he wanted to ignore all the voices in his head telling him not to do anything and jump head-first into something crazy.

Jackson followed her car toward the inn, letting his heartbeat slow down as they pulled into an intersection. He knew he didn't really need to follow her to make sure she made it home okay, but he still wanted to. Plus, it was on his way home anyway, so he wasn't really doing anything extra.

The alpha in him scoffed.

Sure, that's the reason.

Honor pulled out into the intersection, and Jackson drove up to the stop sign just as a dark van barreled into the side of Honor's car.

Holy shit.

The sound of bent metal and tires screeching echoed through the air, the smells of burned rubber and hot metal attacking his senses. Before Jackson could blink or react, the van pulled away, driving like a bat out of hell, its front end damaged. It was too dark to make out a license plate, but he did his best to put the van in his memory.

Honor's car lay in the drainage ditch on the side of the road, the car practically bending inward on itself. Jackson jumped out of his car, his heartbeat a fast echo in his ears.

"Honor!" he yelled as he took out his phone. He dialed 911 as he ran, praying she'd be okay.

"Jacks?"

He almost passed out at her voice.

Thank God.

She was alive.

He told the emergency operator where they were and what had happened then hung up, knowing he needed to put all his attention on Honor. The ambulance would come quickly.

"Honor, baby. Don't move."

He skidded down the embankment and made his way to her door, which was crushed inward and almost faced the back door because of the way the metal was twisted.

His gut clenched, but he ignored it.

She had to be all right.

"I'm fine, Jackson. The airbag saved me I think." Her voice was shaky, but she sounded alert.

"Just humor me then, baby."

She sat in the driver's seat, blood running down her face from where the airbag had hurt her, but he couldn't tell where else she was hurt.

"Honor, talk to me," he asked as he took off his button-down shirt to press against her forehead gently.

"Ouch," she said with a smile. "I'm fine. Really. Just that cut I think." She held back a wince as she tried to move. "Maybe some bruising too."

"Don't move, Honor. We don't know what could be wrong internally. I don't see any evidence of broken bones, but I can't tell from this angle. Please, baby, just sit still."

"You must be scared, Jacks. You keep calling me baby."

He closed his eyes and prayed for patience. "If you're able to make fun of me, you must be fine, but let's pretend you're actually as scared as I am. Keep still."

She didn't move her head, but her eyes met his. "I'm scared as hell, Jacks, but you're here, so I know I'll be okay."

Well, hell. He'd do something with that statement later. First, he had to make sure she was okay.

The sounds of the sirens in the distance were getting closer, and Jackson let out a breath of relief. "Help's on the way."

"I know, Jacks. Did you see who ran that stop sign though?"

"No, not really. It was a dark van, but I didn't get their license plate number. We'll deal with that once you're safe though. What hurts, Honor?"

"Just my head and my side, but I'm okay other than that."

"We'll see what the doctor has to say."

"Jackson?" Tyler called from behind him. Jackson didn't turn to his brother, needing to keep his eyes on Honor.

"We're here, Ty."

"What the hell happened? Who's hurt?"

Jackson told Tyler what he knew, and as the ambulance and fire truck came and used the Jaws of Life to get Honor out of her car, his pulse finally stopped racing.

He got in the back of the ambulance with her against her protests and told his brother to bring his car to the hospital. There was no way he'd let Honor out of his sight right now—despite the rumors that would surely circulate.

Who the hell cared?

He'd almost lost Honor tonight. Hell, if he hadn't said he'd follow her...

No, he wouldn't think about that.

He'd make sure she was okay then figure out what to do with these raging emotions of his because the thought of losing Honor was more than he could bear. Considering he'd told himself he didn't want her for so long, he'd have to think about what that meant.

Then he'd find who'd done this to her and make sure they paid.

CHAPTER 6

"I really don't need to stay at your home, Jacks," Honor said for the eighth time the next morning. Her head ached, but really, all she wanted was to go lie down. Alone.

"Don't argue," Jackson said as he opened his front door for her. "The doctor said you needed someone near you to make sure your concussion doesn't have any adverse side effects, plus, with your bruised rib, you need someone to help you."

They'd spent the night in the emergency room after her hit-and-run. After countless tests, eight stiches, and some binding on her ribs, she had been more than ready to leave.

Then, of course, Jackson's brother, Tyler, had wanted to question her.

Finally, after telling him what she'd seen—which hadn't been much—he'd let her go, but only on the condition that someone could watch her as she slept.

Jackson had volunteered and explained that she'd be staying at his home while she recuperated. She would never get the flabbergasted looks of the hospital personnel out of her mind. Nor would she forget Tyler's knowing glance.

Damn Cooper men.

"I just don't want the town talking about the fact that I'm staying here with you. Alone."

She shuffled into the house and sighed. It looked exactly the same as it had when they'd been together before. The foyer opened up into a beautiful living room that held two large couches and a couple of comfy chairs. The fireplace was built into one wall with bookshelves surrounding it—all dark and prominent—but Honor had always found them beautiful with the hand-carved details.

The kitchen and dining room were to the right off the living room through wide, open

CARRIE ANN RYAN

doorways. She had a feeling he hadn't changed anything in there either, meaning everything would be immaculate and beautiful...even though she had a feeling Jackson didn't use the kitchen as often as he'd like.

If she remembered from what Jackson had said in the past, the Cooper brother who liked to cook the most was Justin, and since he didn't live there anymore, the kitchen might not be put to good use. The image of what the home would look like bursting to the brim with Cooper brothers and their families filled her mind, and she smiled.

The place was the perfect size to hold the five big Cooper men and their growing families. Only she knew that the brothers didn't do dinners there every day, meaning Jackson was alone a lot of the time.

She shook her head then jumped as Jackson placed his hand on her hip then moved to stand in front of her.

"Why are you frowning?" he asked. "What's wrong? Do you hurt? What can I do?"

"Just thinking about how much I like your house."

He looked over his shoulder then back at

her. "Then why were you frowning?"

She smiled and leaned into him, telling herself it was because her head hurt, not because she wanted to be near him. "I guess that didn't make sense, huh?"

He ran his hand down her back, and she closed her eyes, savoring his touch.

"Do you want to go upstairs?" he asked, his voice husky.

She opened her eyes as she looked up at him, unable to say anything.

Jackson grinned and kissed the top of her head. "I mean, do you want to go upstairs and lie in the guest bedroom, or do you want to lie on the couch down here?"

She lowered her head, her cheeks burning.

Well then.

"You have to wake me up every hour, right?"

"Yes, so I think it would be best if you were upstairs. That way you could at least be comfortable while you get no sleep."

She rolled her eyes then nodded. She winced as a flash of pain speared at her.

"Okay, no nodding or quick movements for you," Jackson said as he picked her up, cradling her to his chest.

"What are you doing? I can walk." Even as she said it, she inhaled his masculine scent. He might have been up all night and smelled vaguely of a hospital, but underneath it all, he smelled of Jackson.

Okay, maybe she'd hit her head harder than she thought.

"I want to carry you."

"Well, I guess I won't complain too much then."

He carried her up to the guest room and set her on the large queen bed. She spotted her luggage near the dresser, and she glared at Jackson.

"How did you get all my things?"

Jackson shrugged. "I told you, you're staying here. I had Matt and Jordan get your things and bring them over here. They also closed down the inn since Connie's out of town."

"So he went through my stuff without asking?"

Jackson let out a breath and sat down on the bed next to her. "You weren't completely unpacked so it was easy. Yes, he had to look at some of your things so he wouldn't crush them or screw up your organization."

"I could have taken care of it." Everything was starting to slip from her control. Her car was totaled, her body ached, she wanted a man who probably wanted something different, and now she didn't really have a place to escape to when things went downhill with Jackson.

Which they would.

Again.

"Seriously, Honor? You're freaking out over someone touching your stuff, yet you almost died tonight."

She closed her eyes and rested her head on the pillow. "I know. I'm an idiot. I can't believe that guy ran that stop sign and drove off."

"I'll kill him when I find him," Jackson growled.

"No, you won't, Jacks, but thanks for saying it. You might act all growly, but you wouldn't kill anyone." At his narrowed eyes, she backtracked. "I'm sure you'd at least maim him though."

He shook his head and looked as if he were holding back a smile. "Get some rest, and I'll come in and intrusively wake you up in an hour."

She groaned and turned on her side carefully. "I don't know if I want to go to sleep knowing you'll be back as soon as I close my eyes."

He ran his hand down her side, and she held back a shiver. She was aching, her side hurt like someone had run her over—close enough—and she hadn't slept in far too long. It really was the worse time to be thinking about the fact that she was currently on the same bed as the man she used to love.

Used to.

There was no way she could still love him considering she didn't even know this Jackson.

At least that's what she kept telling herself.

"Get some rest for me, Honor. When you wake up, we can talk about what we're going to do."

Her heart raced. "Do?"

"With us sharing a place. It's going to be weird since I haven't lived with anyone in a long time, not to mention I've never lived with a woman I think I want to see."

She wrinkled her nose. "Think you want to see? Well, isn't that the most glorious title I've ever heard."

He shrugged, not looking the least bit repentant. "We said last night that we needed to talk. We're not in our teens or twenties anymore. I'm not going to ignore the fact that I kissed you like a man who wanted to do much more than that. Hell, I wanted to do much more than that, but we need to make sure we're on the same page."

"I take it you don't know what that page is." Considering she hadn't even known they'd be looking for pages to begin with, she didn't blame him for not knowing.

"No, but you don't either, so we'll take it slow. The hit-and-run complicates things." He grinned as he said it so she resisted the urge to throw a pillow at him. Plus she needed that pillow to soothe her aching head.

"We'll talk tonight." Then a thought hit her. "Shit. Tonight. My job. We didn't call my aunt."

Jackson cursed. "Fuck. How the hell did we forget to call your aunt? The entire Cooper clan knows you're hurt, and we didn't call your family. I'm sorry, baby." He got up off the bed, and she reached out to him too quickly, sending a sharp spear of pain down her side. "Hey, don't move too quickly."

She bit her lip and took a deep breath. "Don't blame yourself for not calling her. I'm not used to relying on anyone or having anyone rely on me. Give me the phone, and I'll talk to her. Knowing this town, she already knows what happened to me and is waiting for me anyway."

He nodded and handed her the house phone on the bedside table.

Her aunt picked up on the second ring. "It's about time you called, girlie."

"I'm so, so sorry I didn't call. I have no idea what I was thinking."

"You were thinking that you were in a car accident and now have the entire Cooper clan taking care of you. Jordan called me by the way so you don't have to worry. I know you and Jackson have other things to worry about. Namely this new predicament of his and your job tonight."

"Tonight? Oh hell. I forgot tonight was the first night on the job."

"Get some rest, and I'll have Brent take care of it. I'm sure he won't mind as he's been taking care of it for a long time anyway."

She winced at the reminder. "No. I'll take care of it. I'm not as hurt as it seems, I promise. I'm just a little tired."

She heard Jackson grunt and looked up as he glared at her. She'd forgotten he was in the room, but it didn't matter. She had a job to do that she'd been neglecting too long.

"If you're sure you're up to it, dear. You only have a couple stops tonight since it's a slow night. Take Jackson with you though."

"Why would I do that? I thought fairies

worked alone."

"He's a sandman, dear. A brand new one with no choice, at that. You and he will both be working the night. Well, didn't that sound dirty? You know what I meant."

Honor held back a smile at the way her aunt's mind worked.

"I also want him there in case you pass out or another accident happens around you. He's been around to save your life—or at least witness you almost dying—twice now."

Honor frowned. It did seem odd that two major accidents had happened to her since she'd moved to Holiday, but, really, she must be just turning accident-prone. Thank God for Jackson though.

"If you're sure," she said, her mind on what she needed to do and not on what had happened.

"I'm sure. I've already been talking to another sandman I know. He should be in town soon to talk to Jackson about what he can do. I'm afraid it won't be much other than show Jackson the ropes though. I don't know of a way to get out of the sandman work other than retiring, and you know it's at least a ten-year commitment."

Honor nodded, already knowing the answer. Poor Jackson.

He already hated magic and now he was thrust in the center of it with these new responsibilities of his and the fact that she'd told him who she was.

That little bit of excitement that had grown within her when he'd touched her side started to shrivel up. There was no way he'd want to be with her when she was the tooth fairy.

Fate really was a bitch sometimes.

"I'll have someone drop by all you'll need tonight, dear. You'll be fine."

Honor snorted. "You say that as if I know what I'm doing."

"Of course you do. It's all in the blood. You've been ignoring it for so long that you're just afraid. And, no, that wasn't a guilt trip, so stop frowning. Take Jackson with you tonight and show him what it is you do. It'll bring you closer."

The only reason Honor didn't roll her

eyes at that comment was that it would probably hurt her head, but it was a close call.

"Fine. Thanks, Aunt Clementine."

"No problem, hon. And Honor?" Her aunt took a deep breath. "I'm so happy you're okay. Don't scare me like that again, okay?"

Honor swallowed hard. "I won't." She winced. "Can you call Tucker?"

Her aunt snorted. "Already did. He'd be on his way over now if it wasn't for me yelling at that boy. You need to work on your magic and on that man of yours. You don't need your brother lurking about and brooding."

Honor smiled at the thought. "He does do that, doesn't he?"

Her aunt chuckled. "Yes he does. Now get some rest and let that handsome Cooper take care of you. You have an easy night tonight, dear."

She hung up and looked up at Jackson.

"I caught most of that since your aunt isn't a quiet speaker. I guess I'm stuck with this whole sandman gig, huh?"

Her heart went out to him. "For a bit at

least. I'll help you though. Sandmen work with kids and so do I. We can work together. Plus if you're here in Holiday, your territory is smaller than most. That's just how things in Holiday are. I'm sure Justin has a smaller territory with his job with Santa."

He nodded but didn't look convinced. "We also have a field trip tonight I hear."

"Tonight's my first night working as a tooth fairy. I'm sorry I forgot."

"You were a little busy trying not to die, Honor. We're fine. I don't know that I like that you'll be out and about so soon after the accident, but I'll be by your side. You're too stubborn to listen to good sense."

She scowled. "Jerk."

His mouth lifted in a semblance of a smile. "Get some rest, and I'll do the same. I'll watch you prance around in a tutu tonight."

Her eyes narrowed. "No tutu for me. No tiara either."

"Well damn. There goes my image of you in that get-up."

"You're a disturbed man, Jackson

Cooper."

"True. See you in an hour."

They slept on and off throughout the day, and after eating some soup Jackson had heated up, she felt much better. Her head still hurt a bit, but not as bad as it had before. The doctors had said she'd be fine within a day or two as long as she didn't bang her head against a wall or something equally as stupid. Her side hurt if she bent the wrong way, but other than that, she was healthy. Yes, she missed her car, but she hadn't lost her life.

Her aunt had sent over her things for the night so she was ready to go. Unlike the outfit Jackson had joked about, there wasn't a uniform. She'd be wearing black jeans and a black shirt though because she liked to blend in. She picked up the small wooden box in her bag and smiled. Once she held this, those without magic wouldn't be able to see her at all. Her aunt had also packed one for Jackson, so they would be safe from prying eyes. They could keep the boxes in their bags or in their hands. As long as it was on their persons and in the middle of its magical duty, they were okay.

"What's that?" Jackson asked as he strolled in wearing dark clothes that clung to his toned body.

She swallowed hard and pulled her gaze to his face. It wouldn't do to pant after the man when she needed to work.

"You'll see, but you'll have to carry one. The box will keep you hidden from prying eyes and little kids who wake up when you get into their rooms."

Jackson frowned as he took the box. "It would be easier for me to just pull the teeth in my office and collect them there."

Honor rolled her eyes. "Sure, then I could just walk in and take the teeth there. You could send me a bill for the coins as well."

"I was just saying."

"I know, but what the tooth fairies do is important. When I take a tooth, I take a little bit of that child's hopes and dreams with me. Well, not per se, it's more like I borrow them. When they get older, they lose that part of themselves, and that's why we have it on reserve. We're there to make sure that, as kids, they keep that innocence and happiness. When a kid loses a tooth and believes in the tooth fairy, they have the joy that comes with knowing they'll find a coin or dollar bill, thanks to inflation, under their pillow."

"Yeah, but their parents could do that."

"Sure, and because of our magic, the parents believe they are doing it, thereby instilling even more hope into the family. If the parents were doing it, though, that reserve of hope and dreams that we have wouldn't exist."

"You mean an actual reserve, don't you?"

"Yep. Right now it fills a few hundred caves and warehouses, I think. My aunt really knows what she's doing with all of that. We fairies collect the teeth then put them in the box. The box, once we're free of prying eyes, will magically go to the right warehouse or cave and be stored forever. When we're on our mission, we'll be hidden. The box knows these things, I promise. Its presence infuses magic and hope into the world, helping more children smile and keep their innocence."

Jackson looked down at that small box in his hands, and Honor was afraid she'd said too much. This was a man who hated magic, and here she was going on and on about how much magic there really was in the world.

"The world's a lot bigger than I thought,

isn't it?" he said, his words low, his tone a bit sad.

She took a chance and walked up to him, placing her hand on his forearm. "Yes, but that doesn't make you small or different. Just more aware."

He nodded, and she leaned into him, resting her head on his upper arm.

"I'll be okay, Honor. I'm just going to have to get over the fact that my life the way I wanted it—or what I thought I wanted—is over now. Things change."

"Does that make you angry?"

"I don't know what it makes me, other than a little lost. I don't like being lost."

Her heart ached for him. "You're the oldest brother. You're not supposed to like being lost. I'm here though, Jackson. I'll help."

He turned and moved his arm so he could wrap it around her. "Oddly enough, it helps knowing that. Okay, now, what do we do?"

She let herself warm in his hold a bit before looking up at him. "Well, you won't be able to feel it, but right now, since the sun is down, I can feel two little teeth that need me. I know it's weird, but it's a connection."

Jackson nodded. "Tyler and Justin tried to explain their connection to their powers to me before. I never really understood how it could work, but I've seen them do it."

"I'm glad you have them then so this will seem a bit easier. When you're trained as a sandman, you'll be able to feel the kids who need a little more help sleeping or those who need to have good dreams."

Jackson let out a breath. "One thing at a time, okay?"

"Sorry. So, first, the boxes will get us to the place we need to go, so no extra travel. It will transport us to the little kid's room, and then I'll take the tooth and place it in the box. Then the box will give me the money or gift depending on the family, and I'll put it under their pillow. After that, I'll close the box and get out a new box. One box per tooth. The one you're holding is an extra one for the night. That way you're connected to me at all times. When everything is done, the boxes will send us home, then be off on their way to their final destination. In reality, the boxes are the tooth fairies, and we're just the carriers, but people help with the whole mystique, you know?"

Jackson nodded, his eyes wide. "This is crazy."

"Yep." She picked up the little velvet bag that held her other box for the night and gripped Jackson's hand. "Ready?"

"As ready as I'll ever be."

She closed her eyes and concentrated on the connection to the lost tooth. When she opened them, they were standing in a young child's room. A nightlight lit up a corner of the room, but other than that, the house was dark.

"Trippy," Jackson whispered.

Honor smiled but shook her head and placed her finger over her mouth. No one could see them, but the last thing she needed was people to hear them and think their house was haunted. Jackson's brother Matt might have been a ghost once, but that didn't mean she needed to help foster the mystical goings-on of the town.

She did as she'd told Jackson and switched out a tooth for a quarter then they were on their way to the next house. Jackson was silent the entire time but never let go of her hand.

When they were in the second room, Jackson cocked his head to the side.

"What is it?" Honor whispered.

"I don't know," he said. "I'm getting a vibe or something from the next room. I've never felt it before but I just know that I need to go next door."

Honor furrowed her brow but nodded. "Okay, let me take this tooth, and we'll go to the next room."

She quickly took the bicuspid and made her way to Jackson's side. Honor might not know exactly what was going on, but she knew it was important to Jackson that he see this through. She also had a feeling it was his sandman powers coming into focus.

They walked into the next room and found another child, this one older, lying down in bed, his eyes wide with stress.

"Come on, go to sleep," the boy, who had to be in his early teens, whispered. "I need to go to sleep. I have that test in the morning. Counting sheep totally isn't helping."

Jackson looked at Honor and swallowed hard.

She smiled at him and cupped his cheek. "Do it," she mouthed.

He nodded then opened his palm as if not knowing what he was doing. Suddenly a small pouch appeared and he gasped. Honor looked over at the boy, but he hadn't seemed to hear.

Thank God.

Jackson opened the pouch and took out a pinch of dust. He looked at Honor, then straightened his shoulders as he walked toward the bed. She watched as he took a deep breath then sprinkled dust on the boy's eyes.

The boy yawned widely then drifted off to sleep, that little line between his eyes fading as he relaxed.

Jackson looked toward Honor and smiled.

Yes, this was what Jackson was meant to do. She'd never been so proud of him. All children needed help sleeping in times of stress and nightmares. Now Jackson would be able to help in more ways than he'd ever thought.

Her head and side had started to ache by the time they got home. No, to Jackson's house. She had to remember that, though it wasn't as if she had a real home at the moment anyway.

It was only around eleven, so not really too late, but she was exhausted emotionally and physically. She'd done her first night as a tooth fairy and hadn't had any problems. She's also shown Jackson a whole new world—one she knew he hadn't wanted in the first place.

"You ready for bed?" he asked as he wrapped his arm around her waist.

Her eyes widened, and she looked up at him.

"I meant to our separate beds. You're still hurt, and we need to talk about what we want to do. We're not going to do that tonight though."

She nodded, her cheeks flaming. "I knew that."

Jackson moved to cup her face. "I want you, Honor. I want you in my bed and beneath me. Never doubt that, but you're tired. I'm tired. And we need to figure it all out— something we're not going to do tonight."

He lowered her face and kissed her when he finished speaking, and she fell into him. God, she loved his taste.

He pulled back and tucked a piece of hair behind her ear. "Good night, Honor."

"Good night," she whispered, her heart racing.

Oh yes, they needed to talk all right. She wasn't sure if she was ready for what was to come, but she had a feeling Jackson would be there. Now she just had to figure out if that's what she wanted.

CHAPTER 7

"Bend over for me," Jackson whispered against her skin, his hands on her hips as his cock lay against the small of her back.

Honor looked over her shoulder and smiled. "And if I don't want to?"

He grinned then tightened his grip with one hand and slapped her ass with the other. She let out a gasp while her eyes darkened.

"Bend over, Honor," he whispered.

She bent over the couch, her legs shaking. He ran his hands down her back, her hips, cupping her ass, and then the most intimate part of her.

"You like this, don't you?" he asked as he slowly rubbed small circles around her clit.

She sighed and wiggled, moving her legs farther apart. "You know it, Jackson. I love everything you do to me. God, it's been so long."

He pulled her closer so his cock moved against her folds, her wetness making it easy to slide smoothly. Still bent over, she looked over her shoulder. "Aren't you going to fuck me, Jacks?"

"I don't know," he said honestly.

She froze then looked up at him, hurt in her eyes. "Why not?"

"Didn't I just leave you in your room?" he asked. Everything felt a bit heavy, a bit foggy. "If this is a dream, I don't want to fuck you. I want the first time my cock is in you, filling you up until you scream my name, to be when we're both awake. When you're actually you, not just a figment of my imagination."

She pulled back from his hold, her eyes wide. "This is my dream, Jackson. I mean...oh God."

He blinked, and the setting changed from his living room to his bedroom. They were both naked, but he felt as confused as he had been before.

"What the hell?"

"I don't know whose dream this is, but we're both in it, Jacks. You either dream-walked to mine or pulled me into yours."

She reached out to him, and he took a step back. Again, the hurt across her features tore at him.

"I can't touch you, or I'll make love to you right here, right now, and I don't think that's the best thing to do at the moment considering I'm confused as hell as to what's going on."

She nodded, some of that hurt disappearing. "I don't know why this happened other than you don't have control of your powers."

He ran a hand through his hair and grunted. "I don't want powers, Honor."

He heard her sigh and forced his gaze to her, trying not to look below her chin at those breasts that could—and had—easily overfilled his hand.

"Jackson, we need to talk once we wake up."

That sounded ominous. "I thought we'd already agreed to that."

"Yes, to talk about our relationship and what that means, but first we need to talk about what you are."

He hated the way she phrased that. He didn't want to be anything but human. God, he sounded like a petulant child.

"I can't change this, can I?"

She gave him a sad smile and shook her head. "No, Jacks, you can't. I'm sorry this was put on you against your will, and I'd give anything to give you a choice, but I can't. My hands are literally tied here. All I can do is try to explain to you that it's not that bad. I mean, really, Jacks, your entire family is touched by magic and the paranormal, and they're fine."

Images of the fights, heartache, and near misses that had occurred when his brothers had found their powers filled his mind.

"I know you're thinking about what

happened to each of them, but stop it. That wasn't because of their magic. That was because people are cruel and idiotic and tried to gain more power or hurt the ones that they thought had hurt them. It happens with humans daily, Jacks. It's not just a magic thing."

He looked down at her and frowned. He'd never thought about it that way. He'd always associated the violence that had occurred around them with the new powers that had come to his brothers.

"I...I don't know, Honor."

He didn't know much of anything anymore, and that, he thought, was the worst of it for him. He didn't like not being in control. He didn't like his choices being taken away from him.

"We'll get you through this, Jacks, but you have to stop fighting it. You have to stop blaming everything that happens on something you can't change. It'll only hurt you in the long run."

He took a step toward her and froze, remembering they were not only in a dream, but naked as well.

"I suppose we should wake up to figure this out, huh?"

Her body blushed from the tip of her ears to her breasts to those gorgeous thighs of hers. This time he didn't bother hiding his hungry look. Hell, she was beautiful, and his cock ached.

"Okay, buddy, that's enough of that. I'll see you in a bit."

He looked up at her and smiled then froze as she faded away, presumably to wake up. Letting out a sigh, he pinched his arm and found himself tangled in his sheets and covered with sweat.

Of course, his dick was as hard as a rock, and Honor was nowhere to be found.

Hell.

Just as he wrapped his hand around the base of his cock, he heard a knock on his door and groaned. He quickly checked the time and cursed. Well, it was time to get up anyway, but hell, his dick would have to wait.

"Hold up, Honor, let me put on my pants."

He heard her laugh through the door. "Considering I just saw you naked, I'm not sure why that matters."

He pulled up his running shorts and groaned as his still-too-hard dick tented out the front.

"Honor, if you come in here when I'm naked, I'm going to throw you on the bed and finish what we started in our dream. It wouldn't matter that we hadn't talked about what we both want for our future. All I'd want is to sink into that sweet pussy of yours and make you come hard and fast."

His dick throbbed harder, and he had to close his eyes to concentrate.

Good going. Why don't you just talk more about sex and what she looks naked while you're trying to get your dick to go down?

Honor opened the door and popped her head in. "Decent?"

"No, but I'm dressed, so come in."

She rolled her eyes and walked in wearing a tank and very sexy short-shorts. "That's an old joke, babe."

"I am old. Put on my robe behind you."

She raised a brow then bent over to pick it up. He groaned as her ass came in full view and those little shorts rode up.

"That was just mean, Honor."

She tightened the robe around her waist and laughed before bending down in front of him. As she rose up, he swallowed hard.

"Put this on, Jacks. If I have to put on more clothes so you don't jump me, you have to do the same."

He looked down at the shirt in her hand and nodded before pulling it over his head.

"We're acting like teenagers," he grumbled and left the room.

Honor followed him. "It could be depravation," she said as they entered the kitchen.

"I take it that means you haven't dated for a while."

Her steps faltered, and he gripped her elbow to keep her from falling.

"I had meant that we hadn't been with

each other for a while, but no, I haven't dated in a bit. I've been too busy finishing my degree and getting the camp area set up at my old place."

The relief that filled him surprised him. It wasn't as if he hadn't known she would date at some point in her life. After all, they'd broken up for what he thought had been for good, and she'd left. There was no reason that she shouldn't have already been married and had babies running around her.

He ground his molars at the thought then stopped. The last thing he needed to do was hurt his teeth considering they were his business.

"Since we woke up to talk about us, I should probably just ask the question. Are you seeing anyone?"

He blinked then laughed. "No, Honor. I wouldn't have kissed you if I'd been seeing anyone. I wasn't that guy before, and I'm not now."

She smiled. "I didn't think you were, but I couldn't be sure. It's been long enough that you could have turned into that cad."

Jackson started the coffee and then went

to the fridge to get things out for an omelet. He knew Honor couldn't boil water, so it would be up to him to cook them something to eat. Thankfully, his mother had ensured he and his brothers could at least provide some meals if needed, though Justin was better than all of them at it.

Not that he'd tell his brother that.

As he chopped, they skated by the real issues, talking about random things going on around town like the next festival or who the best gossip was and how to avoid her wrath. He knew they'd have to talk about the dream and what happened—what was happening—soon, but he knew it would come.

They sat down to eat after Honor set the table. He knew she wanted to help in some way, but there was no way he'd let her near the stove.

"Stop grinning at me like that," she said after she swallowed her first bite. "Yes, you're an amazing cook, and I love eating your food, but that smile means you're thinking about how I'm not allowed near your stove. It was one time, Jacks. One time."

"You burned the pot, Honor. Boiling

water. Water, Honor."

She rolled her eyes. "That was your fault, not mine."

Smiling, he took a sip of his coffee. "Oh really? How is that?"

"I put the pot on the stove to start the pasta, and you bent me over the kitchen island. It's not my fault that you wanted me when I was cooking."

He remembered pounding into her hard and fast, her little skirt bunched at her waist as he made them both come.

"Oh yeah," he said with a grin.

"There's that self-satisfied smile again, though I probably would have burned something later anyway. It was just a good excuse that time."

"True. So, Honor, what are we doing?"

This was something he was good at—being straightforward. He might be an ass to most people and yell, but he never lied if the truth would work so much better. He wanted to lay out the rules and get things done. There was no use pretending and lying about certain things just because they seemed too hard to talk about.

Well, that was usually the case anyway.

For some reason, with Honor, it seemed even harder to talk about what he wanted than usual.

She set her fork down and took a sip of her coffee. "Well, I thought we were eating breakfast and avoiding the tough subjects, but I'm glad we're not. I don't know what we're doing, Jackson. I didn't come back to Holiday for you."

She looked into his eyes as if she needed him to understand that, needed him to understand that she hadn't wallowed and wept for years. He understood that, as he'd moved on as well—or at least he'd thought he had.

Her words didn't hurt because they were true, but that didn't mean he'd step back now that she was here.

Just the opposite in fact.

"I never thought you had, Honor. I know why you came back, and I don't fault you for wanting to keep your distance when you first came here. We didn't end on the best of terms."

She snorted at that, and Jackson smiled. "I'm sorry for what I did back then, Honor."

"No you aren't," she replied. "I don't blame you though for what happened. I needed to leave to get what I wanted in life, and you needed to stay here because this is your home. We weren't ready to be married and live the small-town life then. I don't know if we ever will be." She bit her lip at the last part, and he reached out to grip her hand.

"Then let's talk about that," he said.

"Jackson, we don't really know each other now. I mean, we're getting to know each other, but we don't know everything."

"No, we don't," he agreed. "We're learning though, and I want to keep doing that."

"Tell me what else you want. You always were straightforward about that."

He crooked his lips up in a smile. "I try. What do I want? Well, I want us to be ourselves and try to be together at the same time. We're too old for labels like boyfriend and girlfriend I would think. I've always hated the term lover since it implies that that's all we are—good in bed. I always thought that we had more than that."

She smiled and squeezed his hand. "That's one of the nicest things you've said. Yes, I'm with you that I hate the term lover when we try to do things outside of bed."

"Like on tables and kitchen islands."

She rolled her eyes. "I meant things other than sex, but thanks anyway. So are you saying you want to try to be together now that I'm back?"

"That's exactly what I'm saying. We lost each other all those years ago because we had to, but I'm glad you're back."

"I'm glad we get another chance."

He stared into her eyes, knowing that this was one of those moments he was supposed to remember, one of those times that would make a difference in his future and his plans.

"I have no idea what's going to happen, Honor, but I want to see it through anyway."

"The town will talk," she said.

"They already are."

The town was probably planning their wedding. The marriage of the last available Cooper in town would be an event to remember if they had anything to say about it.

Not that Jackson was planning on getting married.

Hell, he was just ready to start seeing Honor.

Marriage wasn't on the table.

Not really.

"I'm not living with you, Jackson. Not yet."

Her words brought him out of his thoughts, and he scrunched his brow. "Huh?"

She shook her head and laughed. "I'm going back to the inn to stay. I don't want to live with you when we're just starting out. We might have dated before, so we have some the particulars out of the way, but I want to start fresh. Living with you doesn't really accomplish that."

"Okay, but I want to make sure you're healthy. That's more important."

"I'm fine, Jackson. I'm carless, but I'm

fine."

The reminder that she'd almost died made him want to reach out and pull her close so he'd never let her go.

Hell, when Tyler found out who did it, Jackson would kill the stranger. Well, he'd always assumed it was a stranger, but it could be anyone from town—anyone who'd want to hurt her.

"Stop growling, Jacks. I'm going to go take a shower—alone—after I clean up, so you go get showered first. Okay?"

She picked up their dishes, and he nodded.

After they were ready for the day, they met in the living room so Jackson could figure out what they'd do. He knew he should probably go into work, even if it was his day off, but he wanted to be by Honor instead. Apparently having her back in town and in his arms had changed him pretty quickly.

The doorbell rang, pulling him out of his thoughts.

"Who could that be?" he asked.

"Knowing this town and their curiosity, anyone," Honor answered, and Jackson had to agree with her.

Hell, he didn't want to deal with anyone right now. He glared as he stomped his way to the door. He pulled it open and frowned.

"Who are you?" he asked the stranger.

The man had brown hair and blue eyes. He was also about the same age as Jackson and the same height. The grimace on his face made Jackson want to slam the door in the man's face. Jackson had a feeling nothing this man could say could be good.

"Jackson Cooper?" the man asked.

"That's my name, but that doesn't answer my question."

"I'm Sam. Clementine sent me."

Jackson's eyes widened at the mention of Honor's aunt. "She sent you to help me then?"

"Yep. Can I come in? It's hot as hell out here, and I'd rather not let the town know what I'm doing here. You might be on the outskirts and pretty hidden, but that doesn't keep peeping eyes away."

Sam didn't have to tell Jackson that. "Come on it."

He didn't know this man from Adam, but he had a feeling he could trust him for some reason. Jackson wasn't usually wrong about these things.

"Sam!" Honor said as she ran to the man and wrapped her arms around his waist.

Fuck, it seemed Jackson had been wrong about Sam after all. Now he'd have to kill him.

"It's good to see you, Honor. Isabelle misses you."

Honor looked over at Jackson. "Isabelle is Sam's daughter. He's been married for twenty years to Aurora and has six kids, but thanks for acting all growly over me."

Jackson looked down at his fisted hands then up at her. "I growled?"

Honor nodded, and Sam laughed. "Yes, honey, but that's okay. We'll work on your territorial issues later."

"I'm a Cooper. I will always have territorial issues. So, Sam, what is it you wanted to say?"

Sam's smile faded, and he sat on the couch. Jackson and Honor followed, sitting next to each other across from Sam.

"I'm sorry as hell this happened to you. I'm looking into the identity of the sandman who gave the perpetrator the dust. We'll find out."

"I take it you're a sandman as well then."

Sam nodded. "I'm one of the regents— meaning I'm one of the leaders. What was done to you breaks so many laws it's not even funny. That said, there's no way I can take the power away from you. You have to serve the ten years."

He'd known this already, even before someone in charge had confirmed it.

"I'll just have to live with it," Jackson said, and he felt Honor relax next to him.

He knew she felt bad over it, and he knew he had to find a way for her to stop blaming herself. Maybe if he learned to live with his new life, she'd stop worrying.

"Will you teach me?" Jackson asked

Sam.

The other man nodded. "Yes, though first I need to tell you a few things that might be important."

As Jackson listened, his stomach bottomed out.

Hell, that changed things.

CHAPTER 8

The dream started the same as the first one. Honor stood in the field, her hands fisted at her side as Jackson strode toward her.

"Are you really here?" Jackson asked.

"Yes, it's me. You seemed to have dream walked again."

He smiled at her then cupped her face with his hands. "I'm glad. Does it hurt when I do this? Not touching you, but dream walking with you?"

She smiled. "No, Jackson. It doesn't hurt at all. Though I will say that you should be careful as to who you dream walk with."

Jackson nodded. "I think I've only done it with you, so that must be something, right?"

She reached up and kissed his chin. "That's something alright."

"Should we wake up now?" he asked, looking as if he'd rather stay asleep with her.

"Probably, we have a big day."

Jackson just laughed. "Don't stress. I promise they'll be gentle."

Honor rolled her eyes. "Sure, if you say so. See you soon, Jacks."

"See you soon, my Honor."

She woke up alone in bed, but not in her heart. Hell, it was getting harder and harder to keep herself away from him.

But did she really want to?

"Are you sure I look okay?" Honor asked as she ran her hands down her sundress one more time. She'd chosen the white sundress with a knitted white shrug to go over her shoulders. She'd also worn her cute gladiator sandals. They didn't have a heel and made her the perfect height to fit under Jackson's shoulder.

Not that she'd ever adjust her wardrobe to get closer Jackson.

It might have been a factor somewhere in her mind but definitely not the main one.

"You look beautiful, Honor. Stop worrying," Jackson said as he set out olives, cheese, and other snack foods.

She blushed at his words and quit messing with her dress. There was really nothing she could do. She'd already met the women, and she thought they liked her. Now it was just his brothers.

And their children.

They'd like her, or they wouldn't.

"I thought you said Justin and Abigail were going to cook when they got here."

Jackson grinned at her then took her lips in a soft kiss. She leaned into him before he pulled back. Since they'd discussed their relationship, he was always touching her, kissing her as if he were afraid she'd up and leave again. She wasn't planning on it, but she liked the attention anyway. It didn't hurt that she liked making sure he was still there as well.

"I'll let Justin and Abigail do the cooking today because they asked to and because they like it. As for why I have snacks out, that should be obvious. I have four pregnant women about to invade my home. I'm prepared."

She closed her eyes and held back a laugh. "You sound as though you're preparing for war."

Jackson's eyes crinkled at the corners with amusement. "Did I not tell you the peanut butter incident?"

Unable to hold back her laughter anymore, she chuckled. "Yes, though I don't know why it's such a big deal."

Jackson narrowed his eyes then gripped her hips. "The big deal is I'm about to have four pregnant women who could want any random thing, and somehow, I'll end up being the one to go out and buy it even though I'm not married to any of them."

"You were at the store, Jacks, though they didn't know it at first according to Jordan. I had thought you were just getting off work. It only made sense that they'd ask you to pick up something for them. You're family. I know when I get pregnant, and if Tucker is around, I'm going to bother my brother to no end." She closed her mouth quickly, afraid to see Jackson's reaction to her words. She shouldn't have mentioned being pregnant around him considering that would be moving a bit too fast.

He just grinned. "I've yet to meet Tucker, but I think it would be gratifying to ask him for help—just to annoy him. We'd have to make sure to ask all my brothers at random times in the day as well."

She blinked. Had he just said he wanted to have a baby with her? Or was he at least saying he could picture her pregnant with his child?

Her heart raced, but she just smiled. This was what it meant to be in a mature, serious relationship—even though they'd said they'd only see each other. The future actually meant something beyond what to eat the next day.

As scary as all that sounded, it made her happy.

Really freaking happy.

"You've thought about that?" she asked,

not able to hold herself back.

Jackson just smiled and tucked a lock of hair behind her hair. "It seems I have."

The doorbell rang, and Jackson rolled his eyes. It was good to see him as a happy and playful man rather than the man who had to hold himself together straighter than most.

"My brothers usually just let themselves in these days since they all have keys. On non-family-dinner days, they knock, but now they seem to be under the impression that they might be interrupting something."

Honor blushed hard and closed her eyes. "That doesn't make me nervous at all."

She followed him as he went to the door to let their guests in and wrung her hands together. "I'm not usually such a nervous person, Jackson. I don't know what's wrong with me."

She did know though. This was the first time she was meeting his family as part of Jackson's life. If they didn't accept her, she didn't know what Jackson would do. No, that she did know. His brothers meant everything to him.

He put his hand on the doorknob and turned to wrap his arm around her waist. He leaned and kissed her temple. "You'll be fine. Just breathe."

She did as he said while Jackson opened the door.

Soon the house was filled with Coopers and mini Coopers. Yes, she loved the nickname the women had put on their offspring. Each person had hugged her and greeted her as though she was one of their own. Her head was still spinning from when Justin had spun her around, welcoming her to the family.

She'd quickly been taken from his arms by Jackson, who had a scowl on his face.

It might have been wrong, but she loved that scowl. It was just so...Jackson.

"So, tell us, Honor, how long do you plan on staying in Holiday?" Matt asked as he sat down next to her on the couch, then munched on a cracker.

The Coopers weren't exactly subtle in their match making, but she really couldn't blame them considering Jackson was the last single one. She'd heard that as soon as people got married they had to inflict their bliss on everyone around them. It only made sense that all four Cooper brothers, their spouses, and Brayden's children would attack en masse.

She just smiled at him as Jordan hit him upside the head. "Smooth, honey."

Honor shook her head at the couple and took a sip of her drink. "I'm planning on staying for good actually. I came back because my aunt needs me to run Holiday's tooth fairy program."

"Do you have to wear a costume for that?" Tyler asked, and for some reason, Abigail started cracking up laughing as she stole a piece of cheese off Tyler's plate.

As Abigail was now a harpy because of a curse, she couldn't eat off her own plate or she'd be sick. Jackson had explained that to Honor so she knew that the woman, once she was comfortable enough, would be sneaking snacks off her plate if she wanted.

"Why is that so funny?" Honor asked.

"Tyler was apparently worried his stint as a cupid would include tights and a whole lot of pink," Jordan said as she leaned into Matt's side.

Honor smiled. "And did it?"

"No tights," Tyler answered. "Though there is a bow and arrow...and wings."

"That are pink," Matt said, and Tyler threw a cracker.

"What did I say about throwing food?" Jackson said as he came in the room. Without saying anything to her, he pulled her from the couch, sat down, and placed her on his lap.

Honor raised her brow and noticed his brothers did the same. "You could have just asked if you wanted to sit."

Jackson shrugged. "I wanted to sit here."

Honor rolled her eyes again. The man made her do that too often, but she loved him anyway.

She swallowed hard.

Loved?

Oh hell no, she couldn't be in love with him again already. That did beg the question, though, if she'd ever fallen out of love with him in the first place. Hell, things were moving too fast, and yet, as she looked at the happy couples, their futures ripe with new babies, she didn't think time was moving fast enough.

Jackson rubbed the back of her neck, and she sighed against him. "You're a menace," she whispered.

"That was never in doubt, dear," he whispered back.

She laughed softly then froze as she met the curious gazes of every single Cooper—three kids included.

"Stop staring," Jackson mumbled, and Honor squeezed his free hand.

The last thing she needed was tension due to her presence. Well, any more tension than there already was.

Everyone just smiled, but continued to stare.

"Sorry, Honor," Justin said, apologizing as he wrapped an arm around Rina's shoulders. "We can't help it. We haven't seen the guy smile or act like this since...well, ever. We didn't know you when you were dating him before, so we're a little behind on the whole hazing-of-the-big-brother thing."

"You see, Jackson has been, shall we say,

reluctant to enter the real world of talkative people in the past," Brayden said with a grin as Allison ran her hand through his hair in an unconscious gesture.

"You mean he doesn't like to talk about his feelings like the rest of you do?" Honor said, a little annoyed they were putting Jackson in the spot. "I mean, you big tough Cooper men must love gushing about your feelings, right?"

Everyone went silent, and Honor wanted to crawl under a rock. Here she was defending Jackson when his brother hadn't said anything too mean.

Great way to make a good impression, Honor.

Then Matt started to laugh, followed by everyone in the room—including Jackson.

"I see we won't be allowed to harp on you much," Tyler said with a grin. "Sorry, Honor, we just like to gang up on each other, but we don't mean anything by it."

Honor blushed while Jackson pulled her closer. "Sorry, I don't know what came over me."

"My brothers are just being asses like

usual," Jackson said as he rubbed her side.

"Uncle Jacks said ass!" Lacy, Brayden and Allison's six-year-old, wiggled from Allison's hold to come up in front of Jackson. "You owe a dollar to the cuss jar."

Honor held back a laugh as Jackson sighed. "Fine, but you owe a dollar too because you repeated what I said."

Lacy's eyes widened, and she covered her mouth. "I didn't mean to. I swear." She moved her hands, and her little mouth wobbled.

Jackson immediately moved so that Lacy and Honor were each on his lap on a separate knee.

"Now don't cry, Lace," Jackson soothed. "You didn't mean to do it."

Lacy looked up with watery eyes. "So do I still have to pay?"

Honor bit back a laugh at the hope on the little girl's face. She had a feeling Jackson was being played by the adorable girl.

"Don't look at me with those big eyes, Lace. You cuss, you pay." Jackson kissed the top of her head as he said it, and Lacy giggled.

"Fine," the little girl said as she hopped off Jackson's lap. "Can I go play outside now?"

"If your parents say it's okay then fine," Jackson answered. "I put out the horseshoes so the kids could play if they wanted."

Brayden nodded, and Cameron, Aiden, and Lacy ran out screaming and laughing.

"Horseshoes?" Rina asked with a smile. "I didn't think kids played that anymore."

"I'm sure there's an app for that," Honor said while everyone chuckled.

Jackson looked over his shoulder then frowned. Honor squeezed his hand and nodded.

They sat around the room and talked for a bit while people walked in and out, checking on food or getting more drinks.

"I know this is our normal Cooper dinner, but we need to talk about a few things I've learned this week," Jackson said, and everyone got quiet. "Justin, do you need to check the roast or anything? I don't want to have to repeat things."

Justin furrowed his brows then shook his head. "We're fine for a bit. What's up, Jacks?"

Honor moved so she was sitting next to Jackson, rather than on his lap. Matt and Jordan moved as well so it was a tight fit, but this way Jackson could talk more comfortably.

"As you guys know, someone broke into my house and made me a sandman." Jackson let out a dry chuckle. "God, who knew I'd ever say that sentence."

"Most of us wouldn't have thought we'd be where we are," Matt said quietly, and Honor wanted to hug the man.

As long as they made it feel to Jackson that he was normal, he'd be okay. Being magical wasn't a curse, but a blessing in most cases. Jackson just had to believe that.

"Well, Honor's aunt called her friend Sam, who happens to be a sandman regent," Jackson continued.

"Oh, I know Sam. I planned to call him if you needed help," Rina put in.

"Small world," Jackson said with a wry smile. "Sam explained to me that there's no getting out of it. I'm stuck being a sandman for ten years. Usually people ask for the job and the powers that be work with them for that decade. It's usually not a problem."

Honor gripped his hand, and he rubbed small circles along her wrist. She knew he was freaked out and worried about what was coming, but she'd already told him she'd be by his side through all of it.

"Damn," Tyler said. "I've always known what I would be doing, Brayden too. Justin didn't have a choice, but it saved his life. And Matt, well..."

"Mine was an accident, but it wasn't maliciously done." Matt kissed Jordan's brow, and Honor told herself she'd ask Jackson what Matt meant by that later.

"Well, mine was, and we don't know why yet."

Honor winced at that, but Jackson nudged her.

"Stop it, baby. It's not your fault. Sam is looking for the sandman who would dare give over his dust, but right now, I don't know who would have done this. We'll find out somehow though."

"So what is it you'll have to do?" Abby asked.

"Every night I'll have to go out and help children sleep if they're stressed or need help. It's also my job to give good dreams—not nightmares."

"I'm going to go with him each night since I need to anyway with being the tooth fairy," Honor added in. "Jackson doesn't need to work with each child—just like me. It won't take long after sunset so we'd still get our sleep."

Rina smiled. "I'm glad you two can work together."

"Yes, it's as though you're meant for each other," Jordan said, and Honor laughed.

"Subtle," she whispered.

Jordan grinned. "Just saying."

The doorbell rang and everyone looked at one another.

"That would be Sam," Jackson said. "I asked him to join us and help me explain all of this."

Everyone started talking at once and

Jackson left to let Sam in.

"Did you know he was coming?" Matt asked.

"Yes, but I wasn't sure exactly when," Honor answered. She was glad she wasn't going to be the only non-Cooper during the discussion, however.

Sam strolled in after Jackson and everyone introduced themselves. The other sandman didn't look intimated at all considering he was in a room with other magical creatures and the strong Coopers.

Everyone was talking over one another, asking Sam questions about what had happened to Jackson, and Honor was afraid they'd scare the man away.

"Like I was saying," Jackson interrupted. "I'm a sandman. I'm just going to have to live with that."

Everyone murmured their agreements, and Honor leaned into him.

"That's not all Sam told me though," Jackson continued. "Apparently our Cooper ancestors founded Holiday. Did you know that?"

The brothers looked at each other and frowned.

Sam nodded. "Yes, you Coopers started it all."

"I knew we were one of the oldest families, but I didn't know we founded the town," Tyler said.

"Well, yes, we were the ones," Jackson said, his voice slightly shaky. "Apparently that part isn't in our history books."

"That's not all, is it?" Rina asked.

"No, the Coopers founded Holiday because they needed a place where holiday magic could join," Sam said. "Holiday isn't a mecca of magic by chance. It was purposely done a couple hundred of years ago by our blood. The Coopers were all part of various holidays—like we are now—and then, after a time, Holiday grew to be the mecca. That's why we have witches, ghosts, the Ivory Queen, and so many more. Holiday was founded because of the need for peace in magic, and yet that's not what it is now."

"No, everything's a bit crazy," Jordan whispered.

"You mean we're paranormal, or whatever the hell you want to call us, because we've always been?" Brayden asked as he looked over Honor's shoulder to where his kids were playing.

"You Coopers were always part of the magical crowd," Sam explained. "Not all magical elements are genetic like gnomes and elves." Rina smiled. "What happens is the fact that you all are more magical inclined, means you can be part of the holiday magic. It doesn't mean you necessarily have to be or that you have to be a certain kind. That's why you're all so different within your family."

"It's in our blood," Jackson answered. "That's why we're somewhat immune to evil magics and why we're drawn the way we are now. Sam said, though, that I wasn't immune to the sandman's magic because it's not inherently evil, but something that is good and needed. I don't know why it took so long for it all to come back full circle. Hell, I don't even know if our parents knew about magic."

Honor squeezed his hand at his words. The room fell silent as they all thought of the late Coopers. One day she'd get Jackson to open up about them, but right now, it was about letting the other Coopers know they had a purpose.

"What does this mean for us?" Justin asked.

"I don't know yet, but we need to think of something. Right now everything is a bit haywire, and the town is losing something. We have to do our part, now that we know what our history is."

"The town is known for magic," Honor said. "If we bring in something that isn't magic-related for non-magics, then it will help."

"I take it you're doing that," Tyler said.

"Yes, I'm going to try at least."

"When we figure that out, we'll talk about it more," Jackson said. "Right now, though, I wanted to let you know what I've learned. I don't know what we're going to do with it, but now we know that being a Cooper in Holiday means something more than being watched and popular—though I'm pretty sure we all knew this anyway."

"Well, hell, I always knew Coopers were important," Jordan said. "I mean, you're sexy as hell too."

Honor laughed as Jordan cut the tension in the room. She leaned into Jackson again, and he kissed her temple.

"Thank you for being here," he whispered in her ear.

She looked up at him and smiled. "I wouldn't be anywhere else."

Now she just had to think about how long that would be for...and if she wanted it forever.

CHAPTER 9

"You want to go on a hike?"

Jackson ran a hand through his hair and looked down at Honor, who just smiled at him. The cut on her forehead looked as though it was healing, and she hadn't complained about her head or side in the past two days, but that didn't mean she wasn't still hurting. He wouldn't put it past her to hide it from him so he wouldn't worry.

Too bad. He'd always worry.

He couldn't believe she'd almost died—twice—since she'd been back to Holiday. If he could wrap her in bubble wrap he would, though he didn't think she'd agree to that.

"Jackson, I'm a planner. I organize," Honor said as she put her hands on her hips. "This is my job, and frankly, I'd like to get out of the house."

He pulled her close and framed her face with his hands. "I guess I've sort of locked you away in here, haven't I."

She gave him a wry smile. "Considering the only time I've been out of the house was at night to take a couple teeth and watch you sprinkle sand in kids' eyes, yes. I know you had to work, and I can do most of my things from here, but I'd like to get out and breathe a bit."

Jackson frowned. "I just don't want you to get hurt."

"You can't wrap me in bubble wrap, Jacks."

He could have sworn he blushed, but since he was Jackson Cooper and didn't blush, that couldn't be the case. "I have no idea what you're talking about," he lied. "I would never think to do that."

She raised her brows and pulled her head back. "Really? Why don't I believe you?"

Jackson just smiled and leaned down to take her lips in a soft kiss. "Probably because you're right, but it's not as if I'd ever act on that thought."

Riiiight.

"Sure, dear, whatever you say. Now, I know it's your day off, and you'd probably like to be doing manly Cooper things, but I think a hike can fit that need."

"Manly Cooper things?"

Honor grinned. "You know, working with your hands with your shirt off as the sun shines on your body glistening from sweat."

He snorted and rocked against her. "That sounds like a fantasy of yours and not something I'd do with an audience. I could think of a few things we could do at home though." Her eyes widened as he gripped her ass and pulled her even closer.

They'd been sleeping in separate rooms, even though he knew they both wanted to take their relationship to the next level. He'd been waiting for her to be fully healed, and though his cock was ready to explode, he was glad they'd waited.

He also noticed he'd said the word home with ease, but he hoped Honor hadn't. They hadn't discussed her moving back to the inn, and since she'd been carless, she hadn't had a chance to go out and find a place to live.

Oddly enough, he was fine with that. For some reason, he liked the idea of Honor beneath his roof. Everything seemed less lonely and empty with her there. She filled the room with just one smile, and he didn't want to lose that.

Okay, he needed to breathe because he was now spouting poetry in his head.

"When we get back," she said then kissed his chin. "Come on, Jacks, I want to go on a hike. We can go to our lake." She wiggled her eyebrows, and he grinned.

"That doesn't sound like a bad idea," he whispered then took her lips in a deep kiss. He pulled her flush against him, deepening the kiss even further.

She pulled back, leaving both of them breathless. "Go pack some snacks in my bag on the table, and we'll head out. I need to put on my shoes." She pulled away from him, and he was forced to watch her walk away.

The way her hips swung as she moved made up for the loss of contact at least.

They walked through the Cooper backyard to the trail that ran along the back of the property. They held hands like they were in high school, but he didn't care. He liked having her close.

"Why do you live out here all alone, Jacks?" Honor asked after an hour of walking and talking about nothing in particular.

"What do you mean? This is my home."

"I mean, all your brothers moved away, and now you're alone in the big empty house. Why do you insist on staying when you're out here without anyone near you?"

"This was my parents' house, just like it was their parents' before that. The eldest always gets the house eventually. If life hadn't taken over and ruined everything, I wouldn't be living here now. My parents would be."

That familiar pang echoed in the hollow part of his heart where his parents would have been.

"What happened, Jacks?"

He stopped along the path and sat on a rock, pulling Honor down next to him. "I forget sometimes that you didn't grow up here and weren't here when they died."

"You don't have to talk about it if you don't want to. I'm sorry for asking."

He wrapped his arm around her shoulders and pulled her close. "No, I'll talk to you about it. I need you to know." He swallowed hard. "My parents loved each other very much. Even though some of the people in town have happy endings and marriages that lasted, I always knew that what my parents had was different. They were truly in love—like a fairy tale. They were high school sweethearts like Matt and Jordan, but instead of breaking up like Matt and Jordan did, they married right out of high school, went to college, and had me. They were always hugging and kissing, not afraid to show their five sons that love could really happen."

Honor smiled up at him. "I'm glad you had that."

"Me too. In retrospect, I think that's why my brothers seem to have the relationships they do with their wives. It's all still a bit new, but when the Coopers love, they love hard."

He looked into her eyes and tried to get her to know what he was thinking. He loved this woman, but he knew it was too soon to say the words, too soon to really believe them since they were just starting out. That seed of...something...though was there, and he didn't want to let it go.

Though he'd spent most of his life shying away from relationships, he didn't want to shy away from this one. Was it because of what his parents had? He put that aside for now, knowing that what he had to say next would be hard, but with Honor by his side, he thought he could get through it.

"What happened?" Honor asked, her voice low.

"They were out on a drive. I'd come back home from graduate school for the holidays. Matt was just starting high school, and the rest of my brothers were home from either college or were living here since they were too young to move out. It was snowing hard, but Mom and Dad wanted to make sure they got a few of their surprises done before we were all settled."

He remembered that night as though it was yesterday. His mother had smiled and kissed his cheek. He'd been old enough then to start to be able to hug back again—not like he'd been as a teen who'd shunned his mother's attention. His dad had rolled his eyes and pulled his mom out the door, telling him and his brothers that they'd be back soon.

He remembered the way his parents had looked at each other as if they had a secret that only the two of them knew, as if they were as much in love as they had been when they'd first married.

His father had kissed his mom like they hadn't a care in the world and gotten in their car.

"Tyler's old boss came to the door, this was before Tyler was working there, and we knew something had happened. Everyone knew the Coopers, and it had spread over town before we could even process the words coming out of the man's mouth."

His parents' car had hit a patch of ice, and despite how well his dad could drive, nothing could have saved them from crashing into the icy river.

"They might have made it if my mom's seatbelt hadn't gotten caught." He swallowed hard, knowing he had to get through this part.

"They were only partially in the water, but the car filled up pretty quickly. My dad stayed in the car with my mom, trying to cut her out, but it was too cold. Apparently the water was filling up too quickly for him to get out and call for help. There was no one around to help anyway."

Tears fell down Honor's cheeks, and he pulled her close. "They died from hypothermia relatively quickly, but in each other's arms...just the way they'd left the house."

"Oh Jacks," Honor whispered as she moved to wrap her arms around his waist. "I'm so, so sorry."

"People kept telling me when it first happened that at least they had each other. God, I hated when they said that. All I wanted was my parents to come back. I didn't want to lose both at once. I know I was old enough to be on my own, but I didn't want to be on my own. I know it was selfish of me. I know this. I just didn't want them both gone."

"It wasn't selfish, Jackson. No one deserves to lose both parents at the same time."

"Now though? Now I'm glad they had each other in those final moments. I'm glad they weren't alone and were able to be with each other when it really mattered." He took a shaky breath. "God, Honor, if I ever lost you..."

It was the closest he'd come to telling her he loved her. They knew each other better than most people did because of their past and the past week of being in each other's pockets, but it was still too fast.

"Hey, stop that. I'm back, and I'm okay."

"I was just thinking of the accident on the sidewalk and then the car accident. You've had a couple close calls recently."

"I know, crazy right? I'm fine though. I'm healed and perky as ever, so stop worrying about what could happen and live for the now. Okay?"

He smiled and kissed her softly. "I think I can do that. Let's get going because we're close to the lake."

She grinned at him. "I know what you're thinking. Just because we're going to the place where we used to sneak around doesn't mean you're getting any hanky-panky there."

He raised a brow. "I think I can change your mind."

"Sure, all you have to do is crook your finger, but shut up about it."

He laughed as they made their way to the lake. "I don't think you're right about the crooking my finger thing. If anyone has that power, it's you."

"I guess you're right. Now we'll just have to see what happens when I crook that finger."

Jackson groaned then swatted her on the ass. "You're a tease."

"True, but I'm your tease."

Jackson liked the sound of that. They made their way to the lake, and Jackson stopped at the edge to take a deep breath. The sun beat off the water, making the blue even bluer and the water look even more enticing. Maybe he'd convince Honor to go skinny-dipping later.

The thought of her naked with water running down her full breasts made his cock hard, and he groaned.

They were all alone, and he knew no one came around this area of land, so he could have his way with her—and she with him—if they wanted.

"Jackson?"

He turned away from the lake and about swallowed his tongue.

Honor stood naked on a blanket under a tree, a wicked smile on her face.

"Jesus," he whispered.

"I was going through ways of trying to seduce you in my head and came up short. Will this do?"

"Fuck yeah," he said and practically ran as he tore off his clothes.

Honor laughed and shook her head. "Don't trip. Here, let me help you." She knelt before him and untied his boots and took them off.

He took a deep breath, trying to slow down his racing heart. This was Honor, for fuck's sake. They'd made love countless times before—in this very spot in fact—and this wasn't any different.

Yet he knew it was. They were older, and she wasn't leaving.

This meant something beyond a good time, and they both knew it.

She looked up at him, kneeling at his feet, and smiled before undoing his pants then pulling them down his legs along with his boxer briefs. He moved so she could take them fully off then cupped her cheek.

"God, you're beautiful."

She sucked his thumb into her mouth, and he groaned. His cock stood at attention, and he gripped it at the base so he could slowly trace the seam of her lips with the tip.

She opened her mouth, and he sucked in a breath as her tongue darted out to lick the seam.

"Fuck. I'm not going to last long with you in this position. I want to taste you." He pulled away then lay down on the blanket.

"I wanted to suck your dick, Jackson. You can't just leave a girl hanging like that."

He laughed as she tried to pout but smiled with him. "Oh, you're gonna suck me, but I'm going to taste that pretty pussy at the same time. So come straddle my face and suck my cock."

She blushed at his graphic words, and he ate it up. He wasn't usually so wordy while they were going at it. He hadn't been since he'd been with Honor the last time. Others wouldn't be able to handle him, but he knew Honor would.

He knew Honor loved the darkness and touch just as much as he did.

"You have it all planned out, don't you?" she asked even as she moved toward him.

"Yes... no... give me that pussy."

She straddled his face, facing away from him, and bent so all he saw was her pussy.

Seriously. Best. View. Ever.

He gripped her ass and spread her then licked her core, her body shaking as he did so. He licked and sucked, closing his eyes at her sweet taste. He sucked in a breath as Honor licked up his cock then sucked him down, humming along his length as she did so.

Jackson nibbled on her clit and hummed, knowing the vibrations would send her over. She came hard against his face, and he licked up everything he could. Then he moved her off him and onto her back so he wouldn't come.

"Jacks, why did you stop?"

"I don't want to come down your throat—not when I can come inside of you. Now get on all fours because I want you from behind."

"You sure are bossy," she teased, and he rolled her nipple between his fingers, causing her to gasp.

She rolled and looked over her shoulder. "You know I've missed this."

His heart stuttered, and he gripped her hips. "I've missed this too."

"I'm on birth control and clean. We don't need a condom if you don't want."

He swallowed hard and squeezed her hip. "Shit, I forgot a condom. It's in my pants, but we can go without. We've never done that before."

Insecurity filled her gaze, and he cursed himself as she whispered. "I mean…"

"No, I want to be bare in you, baby. I'm going to be bare."

She smiled, and he smacked her ass.

Hard.

Her eyes darkened then narrowed. "What was that for?"

"I saw you liked it in the dream, and I wanted to see if you would still like it when I could actually feel your skin."

He smacked her again, and she wiggled her ass. "You are so not tying me up, mister."

Jackson shook his head and moved so his cock touched her folds. "No, I won't do that. I'd rather have your hands on me. I just like seeing that pretty blush all over that white skin of yours."

She smiled at him, and he slammed in to the hilt.

"Fuck," they said together.

"Jesus, you're tight." He groaned.

"It's...it's been a long time."

He pulled out and cursed. "Baby, you should have told me. Did I hurt you?"

"Fuck me, Jackson. Please. I want you," she pleaded.

Jackson leaned over and kissed her shoulder then her lips. "Anything you want,

Honor. Anything you want."

Still crouched over her, he pivoted his hips, fucking her hard as he kept his lips on her skin, falling in love with her taste all over again.

His hands roamed her body, cupping her breasts, her mound, her hips. His balls tightened, and his cock got even harder until he could barely see, but he couldn't come yet, not when Honor still needed to one more time.

He reached around and stroked her clit once then twice until she cried out his name and her pussy tightened around his dick. He came right after her, filling her up with his seed. They both fell to the blanket, and he turned so they spooned each other, his cock still nestled inside of her.

"Hell, Honor. I think you killed me."

"Any time, Jackson, any time."

He kissed her neck then tangled his fingers with hers, letting the sun heat their already overheated skin and listened to the birds chirp and the wind slide through the trees.

This was what he'd been missing, and he'd be damned if he let it go again.

He just needed to make sure Honor understood that.

CHAPTER 10

Honor stretched her arms over her head, her body deliciously sore from the afternoon before and the prior night when Jackson had shown her exactly how he felt about her. People might say that sex didn't have anything to do with feelings, but she knew better when it came to what she and Jackson had done.

The words would come—from both of them—but for now she was fine living in the moment and knowing that possibilities were out there.

The papers and contracts in front of her, however, needed her attention more than daydreams of a sexy man who knew just how to growl to send her over the edge. Everything was signed by the council and by Jordan. Her next part was to hire builders and developers. It would be a big project and take years to complete, but this is what she loved.

Her breasts ached, and she groaned. Great, now she was horny, and Jackson was at work for the morning. He'd be back later though...

Crap, no, Jordan and Matt were coming over so she could talk to Jordan about her plans for the family camp.

When she'd lived in northern California, she'd started a camp that focused on getting people outside and enjoying their own environment safely and responsibly. There were dozens of parks around where she'd lived, and she'd worked together with them to form an eco-savvy plan where people could not only enjoy the outdoors but also save a tree at the same time. People could come for a day, or stay for a week. She wanted to do the same with Holiday.

The town was dying, and everyone knew it. There wasn't a university or large corporation that had jobs to bring people in. Honor was actually glad of that since she liked the town the way it was.

Holiday just needed a better way to promote itself, and Honor thought they could use tourism to do that. She wanted to use the name of the town itself and bring people in to enjoy different festivals that centered on a holiday while saving the area as well.

Plus, since the town was a paranormal hub, she wanted to bring in people who had their own magical powers so they would know it as a safe haven.

That last part would come later though, and she had a feeling the Coopers would be the center of that. They'd have to find a way to either come out to all of Holiday, or hide themselves. She wasn't sure what they would do, but honestly, that wasn't her decision. She was there to ensure that it could happen if needed.

If they worked together, the town could flourish as a tourist area that centered on the outdoors and holidays. Plus the magical people who came to town could help keep the existence of magic a secret. If more people worked together as a unit, it could work. The people of Holiday already knew a few things beyond ordinary existed. Honor wanted to keep it to that few though. There was no hiding some of the things that had happened in town and frankly, she didn't think they needed to hide everything. Not in Holiday.

What she could do now was in order, and she knew she had an idea that could work. She just had to get it done. There would be more things coming later, and she was happy she was on the right track.

The door opened, bringing her out of her thoughts of Holiday's future and how it meshed with her own, and she smiled. Jackson walked in with two iced teas in his hand and a scowl on his face.

Call her crazy, but she loved that scowl. It meant that something wasn't going according to his very straight-edged plan and that he could allow himself to appear frazzled.

Jackson needed that.

She took a glass from his hand and took a drink. "Thanks. I needed that."

Jackson sat next to her at the table and took a sip of his own. "It's too hot outside to do anything. I know I've been at work today, but hell, it's freaking hot."

Honor just rolled her eyes. "You've just been cooped up in your air-conditioned office all morning. You'll get used to it once we're outside more."

Jackson just frowned and took another drink. "You know that I've done the landscaping around the house and that I can do more with my hands than work with people's teeth, right?"

The thought of just how the good the man was with his hands entered her mind, and she blushed.

Jackson chuckled and reached out to grip her hand. "That's not what I was talking about, but I'll take that blush as a good sign."

"Shush you. Don't act all cocky."

"I thought you liked my cock," he teased.

"You're horrible, but I like you anyway. Yes, I do know you do work outside and don't complain. You're a manly Cooper man, so this has to be about something else."

Jackson sighed and set down his drink. "I just feel like something is off, you know? We don't know why that flowerpot fell when it did, and we haven't found the guy that ran you off

189

the road."

Honor's eyes widened. "You think it's all connected?"

Jackson turned her palm up and traced the lines, as if lost in thought. "I don't know, but I don't like the thought of you hurt."

"That's why you don't like me outside," she said as it dawned on her. "You want me to stay inside in this cocoon until we figure out what's going on. Jackson, we don't know if they were connected, and I don't think they were. Plus, how is me staying inside and never seeing the outside world helping anyone?"

"I told you I'd wrap you up in bubble wrap if I could."

Honor rolled her eyes. "No, actually, I told you I'd never let you do that. You, apparently, had just thought it. I'm fine."

"I hate that word."

"Fine?"

"Yeah, because fine means you're not fine, but you want me to stop bothering you about how you're really feeling."

Honor snorted. "I see that old age has

helped you understand women a bit."

"Watch the age remarks, dear. Considering what we did last night, I wouldn't call me old, would you?"

She fought back the blush and met his gaze head-on. "Oh really? I might have missed some of that. You might want to try again to make sure you did it right."

Jackson growled, and soon she found herself with her back on the table and Jackson between her legs, her sundress riding up along her hips.

"Jacks, Jordan and Matt will be here any minute."

Jackson grinned. "Then I guess I better get to my first course quickly."

He slid his hands up her thighs and gripped the edge of her panties.

"Don't tear them. I need them so I have something on underneath my dress when your brother gets here."

Jackson lowered his head and nipped at her hip, licking along the edge of her panties. "I kind of like the idea of you bare underneath your dress and only we'd know it. That way, whenever we're alone, I can bend you over and fuck you hard until you scream my name."

Heat washed over her as her pussy ached at his words. "I'm not going naked with your family around." She panted as he slowly pulled her panties down her legs.

"That sounds okay to me. Maybe I'll just make you go bare when we're all alone. That way I'll know you're always ready for me."

His voice rumbled against her skin as he spoke, and she closed her eyes so she could focus. The sight of his dark hair between her legs could make her come before he even touched her.

"I think I like you all take-charge," she said.

"Good, because I'm not stopping anytime soon. Put your hands above your head, baby."

She grinned and did as he said. "Why?"

"Because whenever I have my mouth on your pussy you always like to press my head closer. Don't get me wrong. I think that's hot as hell, but right now, I want to be in control. So keep those arms up, and I promise I'll make it worth your while."

"I know you will, Jacks."

She kept her eyes closed, loving the way it enhanced Jackson's touch. She felt his fingers part her folds and jumped as he blew cool air on her pussy. His fingers traced her entrance then he licked her clit.

"You're so wet, baby."

She squirmed on the table and let out a gasp as he slapped her pussy. "Don't move. You're mine, and I'm going to lick and taste every inch of this sweetness until you're screaming my name."

She nodded and bit her lip so she could concentrate as he sucked on her clit, slowly circling around the little nub with the tip of his tongue then taking long licks. Little shocks of pleasure shot through her as he hummed against her clit, her inner walls clenching around three of his fingers. He curled his fingers, pressing against her bundle of nerves, and she sucked in a breath, not wanting to come yet.

His other arm went up beneath her dress, and he cupped her breast through her bra. Between that touch and the vibrations from his humming, she couldn't hold back anymore. She came hard against his face, rocking her hips so she could ride out the bliss. Her nipples pebbled, aching for his mouth, and her inner walls clamped around his fingers. She moaned his name, her body heating.

"That's right, baby. Damn you look like a fucking goddess when you come."

She opened her eyes at his words and almost came again as he licked his fingers one by one, his gaze never tearing from hers.

Honor swallowed hard and tried to speak, but nothing came out. She just looked down his body at his cock that strained against the zipper of his jeans.

Jackson let out a chuckle, and she looked back up at his face. "Matt and Jordan will be her any minute, but as soon as they leave, I'm going to sink my cock into that hot pussy of yours and fuck you hard."

She smiled and sat up. "I'd rather swallow you first."

Jackson groaned and ran his hand through her hair. "That's an image that's going to get me through the rest of the day, baby. I love you at my feet, taking my cock in that pretty mouth of yours."

She reached out and traced the outline of his erection through the denim. "We have some time—"

The doorbell rang, cutting her off.

Jackson kissed her softly, and she blushed at the thought of where his mouth had just been. "Put your panties back on and get yourself calm. I'll go let them in."

"You're flushed too, Jacks," she said as he moved back and she hopped off the table.

"True and I don't think we'll be hiding what we did, but I don't really care."

"Go get your brother," she said before kissing his chin.

He smiled and walked out, a little limp in his step. Apparently he wasn't as calm as he tried to act.

Good because she was about to melt in a puddle at his feet, and this was so not the time for that.

"Hey you," Jordan said as she walked in, her belly a little more pronounced than it had been before. Or at least it looked that way to Honor. Only a week had passed, but Jordan looked happy.

"You're showing more now," Honor said by way of greeting.

Jordan threw her head back and laughed, and Honor blushed. "I think you're the fifth person who's greeted me that way today."

Honor winced. "Sorry. I guess I should have started with hello."

"And worked your way up to my size?"

"Oh shush you. You're beautiful, and you're supposed to gain weight."

"Oh, I know this. As do the rest of the girls, though when I can't button my jeans, I might have to whimper a little bit."

Honor just smiled and shook her head. "At the end of all of this, though, you get a new baby. All of you do. How awesome is that?"

A pang of jealousy hit her, and her smile wavered. She knew she and Jackson were at a different point in their relationship than the other Cooper women, but it still hurt a bit that she wasn't pregnant with the rest of them. It made no sense why she would feel left out, considering she wasn't even married to the man and had just started dating him again, but being the only woman connected to a Cooper man who wasn't pregnant left her at a bit of a loss.

"Hey, you okay?" Jordan asked, and Honor nodded.

"Oh, sorry, just lost in thought over what all needs to be done with work," Honor lied.

Jordan narrowed her eyes but didn't say anything about Honor's obvious subject change. "I'm excited to see what you have. I'm really just the honorary mayor until the new election in a couple months. I'm not running, but I still want to make sure I'm doing the job right while I'm here."

"You'll have to tell me that story sometime."

Jordan grimaced. "Ugh, I hate that story, but sure. Right now I need to pee because apparently that's something I get to do every twenty minutes from now on. I know people say this doesn't happen until later in pregnancies, but I can't help it. Then we can go out to the lake area you're using. I cannot wait to see it in person now that I've seen the plans."

Honor blushed as she thought about how she and Jackson had used that area earlier, but she didn't mention that to Jordan. As close as the Coopers were, the other woman didn't need to know everything about her sex life.

The fact that she actually had a sex life though made Honor want to jump up and down and do some fist pumps.

Not that she'd ever do that.

In front of people.

"I have no idea what you're thinking about, but I think I like it," Jordan teased, and Honor blinked.

"Oh, sorry. Uh, what were we doing?"

"After I get back, we're going to go out and see the site where you want to build this center."

"Sounds good to me, though should you be hiking in your condition?"

Jordan rolled her eyes. "This is more of a walk since we're taking the trail, but yes, I'll be fine. No mountain or rock climbing for me."

Soon they were on their way to the lake, each couple walking side by side and enjoying the late afternoon air. There was finally a slight breeze, and Honor was in love with it. They spent another hour going over the logistics of building the camp and how the traffic would be changed with the new addition. There was already a road that led to the lake, but it was rarely used because there was another lake on the other side of town that was closer to the amenities like the inn and other places they'd build in the future. Honor could have planned on building near that one, but this lake had always held a special meaning for her.

She blushed at just how special it was but didn't look at Jackson.

She wasn't sure what she'd do if she met his gaze.

"So I take it you're going to have rock climbing?" Matt asked, pulling Honor out of her thoughts.

"Yes, but it won't be invasive. We'll have the indoor wall for people wanting to learn. We won't let them climb without certification. That's the way it is now, so we're not going to change that."

Matt nodded and glanced at the rocks ahead of them. "I haven't been rock climbing in ages. I know Tyler still does it when he gets a chance. This might be great if I wanted to try it again."

Jordan wrapped her arm around his waist. "You're going to have to be really, really careful. I know I'm the tough one, but propelling down a rock face scares the crap out of me."

Matt kissed the top of her head and pulled her close. "I'll be careful, don't worry."

Jackson came up behind Honor and put his arm around her shoulders. She leaned into him to inhale that sandalwood scent she loved but didn't say anything.

"You better be careful," Jackson said. "Our family has had enough excitement recently."

Matt and Jordan nodded while Honor repressed a shiver. She might not have been here for all of their adventures, but their close calls, combined with her own, made her want to be extra careful. Add onto that the fact that someone wanted to hurt her through Jackson and she really needed to be cautious.

"You okay?" Jackson asked softly.

She looked up at him and smiled. "Yes, I was just thinking about what's been happening recently."

"I'm going to go take a look at the rock face," Matt said, breaking Honor out of her thoughts. "You took measurements, right?"

Honor nodded. "Yes, and I'm having professionals come out and do everything. I'm just the planner."

Matt smiled. "Wanna show me what you're thinking? I know I can't help, but I'm excited." He turned toward Jordan. "I'd rather you stay here, baby."

Jordan narrowed her eyes but smiled. "I know you're thinking I'm the pregnant woman who needs to stay still, but I'll let you get away with it this once. I'm not in the mood to trip and fall over those rocks anyway."

Matt grinned and kissed his wife while Jackson kissed Honor's temple. "I'll stay here with Jordan to talk about the other things she's going to need to do to help you out."

Honor laughed. "You mean watch her so she and the baby are okay."

"That too. She's having a Cooper baby after all."

Honor rolled her eyes while Jordan laughed.

"You really do marry all the brothers when you marry into the family, Honor," Jordan teased then froze while her eyes widened. "I mean..."

Honor shook her head. "I know what you mean. No pressure, right?" She smiled through her words, even though her heart sped up at the thought of being with Jackson forever.

That was something they'd have to talk about later.

She led Matt to where she was planning on having the climbing area, leaving Jackson and Jordan behind.

"So, how serious are you and my brother?"

Honor snorted but didn't look at him, making sure she kept her eyes on her path so she wouldn't trip.

"Subtle, Cooper."

"I'm not really good with the intrigue."

"Did your family nominate you to ask?" She climbed up on one of the rocks, and her legs shook. Damn, she needed to get in better shape apparently. Or it could have been the conversation she was having.

Matt gripped her arm to steady her then stepped up beside her. "No, actually, we all decided whoever got you alone first would ask."

Honor rolled her eyes.

"I don't know what exactly will happen in the future other than I plan on doing what we're doing now. I...care for Jackson."

"I heard that hesitation there."

"If and when I do say something along the lines of something more, I'd like Jackson to be the first to know. Okay?"

"Sounds reasonable. I know it's a little intimidating to be with a man who has family such as ours, but, Honor, I want you to know we like you."

That little spot in her heart where the fear of rejection had taken root started to warm again. "I'm glad you like me, but don't put all your hopes on me. It's a little daunting."

"He's never been with anyone like you before. He's never looked at anyone the way he looks at you. He's different with you. I mean, we always knew he wasn't the cold man he portrayed, but you're breaking through that so everyone can see the man he is—not the man he wants to be seen as."

She nodded at his words but didn't say anything. While it was nice that Matt and the rest of the Coopers knew that Jackson was more than a scowl, she didn't like the added pressure of being responsible for showing who he was.

It wasn't Jackson's fault he didn't want to conform.

"Do you think—" Honor cut off at the loud cracking sound that echoed through the air.

The hair on her arms rose and she looked up and screamed.

"What the hell?" Matt asked then looked up. "Fuck! Move!"

He pushed her out of the way, throwing his body over hers as large rocks crashed around them. She felt the sharp sting as small rocks hit her and tried to tuck herself into a ball under Matt.

Matt grunted then screamed in pain, his voice blending with Jackson's and Jordan's screams from afar.

"Matt!" she yelled as the rocks stopped falling for the moment.

She moved him off her and swallowed. "Matt?"

"I'm fine." He groaned. "The big rocks missed me, but I think a medium rock broke my arm. You're bleeding."

He was pale, bleeding, and wincing as he tried to move his arm. "Don't worry about me. Let's get you to the hospital, okay?"

Matt grunted and sat up. "Fuck. I'm okay, really. I don't think anything else is broken."

Tears stained her cheeks, but she nodded. "That's good to hear, but let's have a doctor take a look, okay?"

"Honor!" Jackson yelled her name as he ran up to her, after he finished climbing. "Oh, baby, let's get you out of here. Matt? You okay?"

"Fine, just a broken arm. I think Honor's stitches broke open though." He looked past Jackson to Jordan, who stood where she'd been before, her cell phone clutched in her hand and tears sliding down her cheeks.

"Jordan's calling an ambulance to come and get you," Jackson said as he helped Honor and Matt stand.

"This is the second time I've been in an ambulance recently," Honor said as she looked into Jackson's eyes.

He narrowed them as he kissed her temple. "These weren't accidents."

"I know."

"We're going to find this bastard, Honor," Jackson vowed.

"He's messed with the wrong family," Matt said as he limped toward Jordan.

She nodded but didn't say anything. Someone had tried to kill her three times since she'd moved to town. Why would someone do that?

Honor bit her lip and tried not to cry at the stress. The fact that someone would want to kill her left her at a loss, but by doing so, they were also hurting those she loved.

She might not have any magical powers to protect herself, but she'd be damned if she let those she loved get hurt again because someone wanted at her.

She'd find this person somehow.

Somehow.

CHAPTER 11

"Still no word?" Brayden asked as he held Cameron's snow cone so the boy could tie his shoes.

Jackson grunted then leaned in to inhale Lacy's sweet little girl scent. It seemed to calm him—even if her hands were sticky and currently patting his head in sympathy.

"No word," Jackson finally said. "Tyler and his crew can't find any evidence on the hilltop other than someone had been there and caused the rock fall. There were footprints and someone had used a crowbar or another thing for leverage to push the rocks down. They still haven't found the van, and there aren't any fingerprints on the windowsill where the flowerpot was that almost hit Honor."

Brayden handed his son back his snow cone and frowned. "We know that the man isn't as normal as other criminals that Tyler chases. The man had magic or knows magic considering what he did with you."

Though they were on the sidewalk alone, Jackson still looked around to make sure they weren't overheard. The people of Holiday might think they knew about magic and all it entailed, but what they knew was far from the truth.

"I'm just sick of this," Jackson said, keeping his voice light since they were in front of the kids.

It had been four days since the rock slide that had almost killed Honor and Matt. His brother had broken his arm and had a few bruises while Honor was fine other than tearing her stitches from the car accident. It could have been so much worse.

Worse enough that he held Honor tight to him every night, not able to sleep. He'd almost thought about sprinkling his own dust on his eyes, but he wanted to be able to wake up at any moment and keep an eye on Honor.

"Don't frown, Uncle Jacks," Lacy said as she kissed his cheek.

A part of him melted at this little girl. Before he'd probably have tried to ignore her and done his duty as uncle by holding her, but now didn't care about keeping up with his grumpy persona.

He kissed her cheek and smiled. "I'm sorry, hon. I'll try to do better."

"I like this side of you," Brayden said as they walked down the street. Cameron and Aiden walked on either side of his brother, in a deep conversation about which comic book character should get the next movie and why.

"What side?"

"This smiling side of you. Honor's good for you."

Jackson grunted but couldn't stop his smile. "Yeah, I guess she is."

"Don't let her go."

"Not planning on it, but don't make a big deal about it. I'm quite happy with how things are going. Well, other than whoever this guy is."

Brayden scowled. "We'll find him."

"I don't really know how other than offering up Honor as bait. And, no, we won't be doing that."

"I wouldn't think you'd let that happen, though I don't think you can hold back Honor if she wanted to try."

"Oh, I'll hold her back." He'd wrap her in that bubble wrap he'd promised then stuff her in a room and never let her out.

Well, hell, he knew he couldn't do that. He'd take the spark right out of her. He loved that damn spark.

"She's stronger than you think."

"I know how strong she is, and darn it, you're right."

He'd just have to be by her side. It wouldn't do to stand in front of her and take the blow or hide her away. Honor was more than that.

They were more than that.

"I just want her to leave. I want to keep

doing what I was doing. I was everything here and now she's back and going to take it all. She needs to go. Is that so wrong?"

Chills ran down Jackson's back as he froze then turned on his heel at the voice.

The man before him looked average. Brown eyes, brown hair, average height, average build. Nothing about him looked remarkable except for the fact that Jackson had seen him before.

In his dreams.

This was the man who'd changed his life.

Changed him into a sandman.

This was the man who wanted to kill Honor—who'd almost killed her three times now.

"Who are you?" Jackson asked as he slowly slid a shaking Lacy down his body.

The little girl might not know what exactly was going on, but the tension in the air was thick enough that she seemed to understand to be quiet. He tucked her behind him in case this stranger attacked. Out of the corner of his eye, he saw Brayden hide Aiden and Cameron behind him.

They were on the wide-open sidewalk, and most of the town occupants were indoors in the high heat.

This was going to be bad.

"Who are you?" Jackson asked again as calmly as he could. He didn't want to get the children hurt because of the crazy man in front of him.

"You don't even know who I am. That's what pisses me off," the other man spat. "I've been here for years working my ass off, and nobody knows. Nobody knows what I've done and how hard it is to work in two regions just because that dumb bitch can't make a decision."

"I'm sorry. I don't know your name, but how about we go sit and talk about that?" Jackson said calmly.

"My name is Brent. Honor knows who I am. Or at least, she should. That stupid bitch should know everything about me."

"How about you watch your language in front of my kids?" Brayden said, his voice smooth. "I'm going to take them back to their mom, and then you, Jackson, and I can talk."

Brent grimaced then reached into his coat—something the man shouldn't have been wearing in this high heat—and pulled out a gun.

Jackson's heart sped up, and Lacy's grip on his leg tightened.

"You don't have to do this, Brent," Jackson said, not as calm as it had been before.

"You think I want to do this? If it wasn't for that bitch, Honor, I wouldn't be in this position. It's all about her and her worries though. She never thinks about the rest of us or about how her going and coming can change everything. You, above all, should know this. She left you alone and look what happened. You became that icy bastard that no one likes."

Jackson's eyes darted around, but he didn't see a way out of this. They stood out in the open with a glass window behind them.

He'd have to talk and find a way to convince the man to let the children go. Hopefully, someone in town would be their nosy selves and look out their window so they could call Tyler.

With all the magic in the world, he didn't have any defense. He was as useless as ever, and he couldn't think of a way to protect his family.

There had to be something he could do.

"Brent, I'm sorry about what happened," Jackson said. "This isn't the answer though."

"You're a fucking Cooper! You're not God, even though the lot of you seems to think you are. You don't get to decide what I do. You don't get to fix this. How hard is it for people to just understand that I deserve something more than a pat on the back and a kick in the ass?"

"I don't understand," Jackson said as he took a step back, shielding Lacy. Brent's eyes narrowed, and Jackson froze.

Okay, no moving.

"Of course you don't understand. Why would Honor explain anything to you? She's the fucking princess and can do anything she wants regardless of the consequences and who she steps on to get there."

"Brent, put the gun away. We can talk about this."

Jackson froze again as he heard Honor walk up from behind him. No, she couldn't be here.

"You bitch! You ruined everything."

"Now, Brent, dear, this isn't the way. You know this." Honor's Aunt Clementine passed Jackson, her head held high as she faced down the man with the gun.

"Stay out of this, Clementine," Brent said.

"No, I won't. Put the gun down, and let's talk about what you're thinking," Clementine ordered in a calm voice.

"You should have noticed me. You should know what I'm talking about."

Honor stood by Jackson's side and gripped his hand. Hell, she couldn't be here. She had to leave. He didn't know what he'd do if he lost her.

She was his life, and he'd just figured it out.

They'd already gotten their second chance, and he'd be damned if he lost it.

"Tell us," Honor pleaded. "Tell us what I

did."

"You left. You left everyone here because you were a selfish bitch. When you left, someone had to take over your territory—the territory you would have been using if you'd done your job—because you couldn't be bothered to do your duty. No one else would have gotten away with it. For fuck's sake, Jackson can't get out of being a sandman because he knows the rules. You, on the other hand, get away with everything. You're the niece of the Ivory Queen, and when you find the time in your busy fucking life, you'll be groomed to take over for her. It's all in the blood, but your blood is dirty."

All of this because Honor had been allowed to take her time and wait until she was ready? All tooth fairies were allowed to start when they were ready, she wasn't special.

She wasn't.

"Honor feels bad about all of this," Jackson said. "She's torn herself up over her decisions, but she was allowed to leave, Brent. She was allowed to find herself outside of her duty."

"Jackson, don't," Honor whispered.

"She's selfish," Brent spat. "I did all of her work and mine for years, and nobody noticed."

"We all noticed," Clementine said. "We did. You know this, Brent. You even told me you were fine with the extra work because you love doing what you do. When Honor came back, you were happy."

"You just saw what you wanted to see. You're nothing. Just like her."

He aimed the gun at Jackson and grimaced. "I tried to hurt her through you, Jackson. Everyone knew Jackson hated Jordan's magic and then everything else that happened with his family and magic. I knew you loved him from before; you can't hide things from me. I knew. I gave you the thing we all know you hated, but you persevered. You weren't supposed to do that. I even had to use my favor from my sandman friend to get that dust. Now that bastard sandman, Sam, found out. He took my friend away and now he's going to come for me."

Jackson inwardly cursed. Sam had found out what had happened and if Brent was freaking out now, that meant Sam had to have been close to finding it all.

It all would have been over safely if Brent hadn't gone off the deep end.

"Now I guess I'll have to hurt Honor another way. I'll be remembered now. I was the golden boy around here until you showed back up. Clementine would have made me her heir. You ruined everything and you now have to go."

Honor moved in front of him, and Jackson cursed.

"Honor, move," Jackson whispered.

"No," she said sternly. "You don't get to hurt the man I love. You don't get to hurt anyone. Brent, if you have an issue with me, then make it with me."

Jackson blinked at her declaration but set it aside. He'd deal with that later. Now he needed to get the woman he loved out of harm's way.

Brent closed his eyes tightly then opened them. "If you're dead, you can't feel the hurt."

No shit, Sherlock.

"That's why I didn't want you dead before," Brent added and Jackson's heart seized.

Where the hell was Tyler?

Jackson reached out and gripped Honor's hip, pulling her back. She wouldn't move to his side, but at least he could feel her against him.

"Brent, I'm sorry," Honor said. "I'm so, so sorry. I was a selfish brat. I shouldn't have gone and finished my degree. I should have stayed here so you wouldn't have to deal with everything I left behind. I'll leave again if you want to keep the region. Or I'll stay and give you all the credit. Just tell me what to do. Don't hurt my family."

Brent screamed and fired.

Seconds ticked by slowly as Jackson gripped Honor to him at the same time leaning down to cover Lacy. Glass shattered behind them as the store window burst.

Lacy screamed, and Jackson looked down at the little girl with glass in her hair but, miraculously, no cuts on her body.

"I'm not joking around," Brent yelled. "Stand up, all of you. Don't move."

Jackson stood with a shaking Lacy on his leg. Brayden stood with his sons behind him, and Honor and Clementine stood between them.

"You don't have to do this," Honor cried, and he squeezed her hand.

He'd never felt more helpless in his life. Not when she'd left him before because she'd had to. Not when he'd pushed Honor out of the way from the flowerpot. Not when Brent ran her off the road. Not when Brent had almost killed her and Matt in the rock slide.

Now he was helpless at the mercy of a mad man who wanted recognition but wanted vengeance just as much.

"I have to. Don't you see? Nothing worked. I wanted you to hurt, and you kept getting better. I wanted Jackson to leave you and blame you for everything. Instead, you two seemed closer than ever. I just want my job back. What's so wrong with that?"

Everything, but Jackson didn't say that. Brent made no sense, yet there was nothing he could do. Not when any action could hurt his family.

"I don't want to kill you, Honor. That

was never the plan, but I don't see another way out."

A single tear slid down Brent's cheek, and he fired. Jackson threw himself over Honor's body, pulling Lacy with him. The silence after the blast was deafening.

Brent screamed, and Jackson looked up to see the other man clutching his hand, blood streaming down his coat. Tyler had the man's other arm behind his back and was reading him his rights.

Hugh, Tyler's deputy, looked a bit shell-shocked but holstered his gun.

It seemed that Jackson had missed the second shot—Hugh's.

He pulled himself up and looked over Lacy and Honor. "Are you two all right? What's wrong? Tell me."

Lacy nodded, tears streaming down her face. "I'm fine, Uncle Jacks. Is the bad man gone now?"

He kissed Lacy's forehead and let himself breathe. "Yes, baby. He's gone now." Or would be soon.

"Lacy!" Brayden crawled over to his daughter and hugged her close. Aiden and Cameron sat on the ground behind him, their faces pale, but otherwise they both looked okay.

Clementine squeezed his arm and nodded. "Thank you for taking care of my baby."

He frowned. "I didn't do anything."

"You've done more than you know. Keep her safe, Jackson Cooper."

He nodded then looked down at the woman in his arms. "Honor."

She gave a wobbly smile then threw her arms around his neck. "Oh my God, Jackson. He could have killed you."

"He could have killed you."

"I'm so sorry."

He framed her face with his hands, ignoring the growing crowd around them. "Never be sorry for another's actions. You did nothing wrong. We've gone over this. This man wanted something to lash out at because he's a small man who doesn't understand that his own actions have consequences. This wasn't your fault."

She kissed him softly. "I love you so much."

Despite everything happening around them, he smiled. "I love you, Honor. I love you so much, and I'm never letting you go. You don't get to find a new place to live because you're by my side. I want to watch you grow old, grow round with our child. I want to watch you work your magic and learn to use mine. I want it all."

Honor smiled. "I think I can agree to all of that."

"Good, because you're my dream, Honor. I'm never letting you go."

He knew the world was waiting. His family needed to know everything. Tyler needed a statement, and the town needed answers, but he didn't care. At that moment, his whole world was the woman in his arms, and he'd be damned if he lost that time.

Honor was his.

His dream.

His magic.

His everything.

CHAPTER 12

"We should wake up, you know," Honor said as Jackson ran his hands up and down her sides, leaving them on her rounded belly.

"Since I've already made love to you in our dreams, I guess it's time to wake up. Though I'm not letting you out of bed right away."

She smiled at him and kissed his chin. "I think I'm okay with that."

"I'm getting better at this dream-walking thing. It only took a year to make sure I didn't do it accidentally."

"You're amazing, dear," she teased. "See you when I wake up."

Honor blinked and smiled as Jackson's face came into view. "Good morning."

"Good morning, my wife," he said, his voice low with sleep. He placed his hand on her belly, and their child kicked. Jackson's eyes widened with awe, and she fell that much more in love with him. "I'm never going to get used to that."

"I love you so much, Jackson Cooper."

"I love you just as much, Honor Cooper."

"Am I getting too big to be on top?" she asked as she ran her hand down his stomach to grip the base of his erection.

He groaned and rubbed her wrist. "No, the doctor said we're fine. Now climb up, baby. I know how much you love when I let you have control."

"Let?"

"You know what I mean."

"Sure, baby. Whatever you say." She moved so she straddled him then slowly, oh so slowly, slid down his cock. He filled her up, and she had to close her eyes to make sure she didn't succumb to bliss too quickly.

"Ride me," Jackson ordered, his voice husky and sexy as hell.

She placed her hands on his chest and moved up and down, setting the pace slow as they woke up. Her breasts were heavy and full, sensitive due to the pregnancy and the man beneath her.

Jackson gripped her hips, keeping her steady, and soon she found herself throwing her head back as she came, him following soon after.

"I'm so glad this is how we wake up every morning."

Honor smiled at her husband's words. "It helps that we set our own hours so we go into our jobs at the same time. This way we get our morning sex."

Jackson chuckled. "Well, it's a perk for sure. Now let's go hop in the shower and get ready. The family is coming soon."

"Make sure you have the peanut butter ready," she called over her shoulder as she made her way to the bathroom.

"I will never understand that craving. How is it that all five of you Cooper women are pregnant? I mean, it was odd as hell the first time the four of them were pregnant. Now they're all pregnant again, and you joined in."

Honor stepped into the shower and laughed. "What can I say? We're weird as hell."

"You're my little weirdo, so I'll take it."

After they were done showering—which seemed to take longer with two people sharing rather than saving water like Jackson always used as an excuse—they finished setting up the downstairs for the arrival of the Coopers.

New stay-at-home mom Jordan and Matt would be bringing appetizers and their daughter, Azalea. As were the rest of them, they were keeping the sex of their next baby a surprise. In a few months, when all the new mini Coopers arrived, it would be a huge party. Honor loved the fact that Jordan was keeping her witchcraft close to her heart and helping others. She'd even taken on a new apprentice so the family magic would never go away.

Justin and Rina were bringing potatoes and another side dish, along with their daughter, Holly. Jackson had given Justin grief over the heavy Christmas name, but considering who her parents were, it only made sense.

Tyler and Abigail were bringing turkey and dressing, along with their son, Eric. While the rest of the Coopers had loved the fact that most of them had had girls, Tyler brought a son into the mix. Honor shook her head at the thought. That man didn't need anything else to prove he was a man's man, but she had a feeling that Abby would be having a girl next. She couldn't wait to see Tyler fall in love and break down over a little girl.

In fact, none of the Coopers could wait.

Brayden and Allison were pregnant with their sixth child—something that Allison wanted to scream over, even if she was happy about it. Apparently Brayden would be getting snipped soon, considering in addition to Aiden, Cameron, and Lacy, they'd had twin girls, Charity and Karen. They were bringing ham and finger foods for the kids, considering they had more kids than the rest of them.

She'd once only had her brother and parents who didn't understand magic and wanted nothing to do with it. Now she was immersed within the Cooper and Holiday worlds. The camp had broken ground a couple months ago and was getting closer to being done. Soon there would be a place for people to enjoy the area, bring more jobs in, and eventually, she'd find a way to open it to the magical. She'd already talked with Rina about how that would work since Rina knew more about the paranormal than anyone.

Things were changing and the Coopers were in the center of it.

Soon Jackson's three cousins, Caleb, Carly, and Chase, would be moving to town due to the death of Caleb's wife. The three cousins wanted to raise Caleb's two children together, so they were moving to the small town of Holiday because family was more important than anything. Even her brother, Tucker, had plans on visiting, if not moving, to Holiday.

The town drew people in, even when they wanted to move away. It had brought her and Jackson together and had brought the Coopers closer than ever.

She'd never forget what it meant to leave and who it had hurt in the process, but she'd learn to forgive. Brent was behind bars, and her Aunt Clementine was teaching her what it meant to be a tooth fairy and queen in truth.

The future was rife with magic and possibilities, and through it all, Holiday was at the center.

Jackson came up behind her and wrapped his arms around her waist. "What are you thinking about that's making you look so serious?"

"Just thinking about Holiday and how it's the center of our lives as much as the Coopers are the center of the town."

He kissed her temple and placed his hands on her belly. "I tried to run away for so long. Not from the town, but from what the town meant. I'm glad you brought me back."

She smiled and turned in his arms so she could kiss his jaw. "You did the same for me, Jackson. You're my everything."

"You're my dream."

"You keep saying that." And she loved every time he did.

"I'd dream-walk through thousands of dreams to find you, Honor. You're my center. You're the one who made me see that a smile is okay—that magic is okay."

She warmed at his touch and looked into those blue eyes she loved. "Holiday's full of magic, Jackson, but right here, this connection between us? That's the magic I want. That's what I need."

He leaned down to take her lips, and she melted.

Honor was a Cooper in every sense of the word, and when the town would eventually move on and find something else to gossip about, she'd still be at the center with her Jackson. She'd found the man of her dreams, and this time, she wasn't letting him go.

Coming in 2016 - The Second Arc of Holiday Montana

Where Make Believe is Real and the Coopers aren't Going Away Any Time Soon

ABOUT THE AUTHOR

Carrie Ann Ryan is a bestselling paranormal and contemporary romance author. After spending too much time behind a lab bench, she decided to dive into the romance world and find her werewolf mate - even if it's just in her books. Happy endings are always near - even if you have to get over the challenges of falling in love first.

Carrie Ann's Redwood Pack series is a bestselling series that has made the shifter world even more real to her and has allowed the Dante's Circle and Holiday, Montana series to be born. She's also an avid reader and lover of romance and fiction novels. She loves meeting new authors and new worlds. Any recommendations you have are appreciated. Carrie Ann lives in New England with her husband and two kittens.

www.carrieannryan.com

Printed in Great Britain
by Amazon.co.uk, Ltd.,
Marston Gate.